The Vessel

Callum McLaughlin

Copyright © 2013 Callum McLaughlin

All rights reserved.

ISBN-10: 149373797X
ISBN-13: 978-1493737970

Chapter One

The smell of metal lingered in the air as water dripped from the broken pipes overhead. The single source of light was that of a bulb dangling from the ceiling in the centre of the room. Shadows swelled ominously upon the damp, grey walls as it swayed to and fro. Echoing footsteps, once distant, were growing ever louder. This could mean only one thing; time for another check-up.

Taking slow, shallow breaths, Eva Cole, the room's sole inhabitant, lay back on the rusted frame they called a bed; the stained mass of springs protruding in all directions digging into her spine. She would have only one chance to do this; she had to do it right.

She clenched her eyes shut in unison with the all too familiar clicking of the door's lock. Head cocked towards the wall, she waited. His breath revealed his identity to her almost immediately; it was Johnson, as it almost always was on a Tuesday afternoon. The stench of stale coffee and cigarettes penetrated her lungs but she refused to move; he had to believe she was asleep.

It took all of her effort not to flinch as the screech of the springs from the mattress struggling to take his weight sent a stabbing sensation through her heart. Perched by her side, he removed the needle from its sheath and - as he always did - tapped the end twice, swirling the red liquid inside.

This was it. She held her breath for three more seconds then threw herself into action. Sitting up and grabbing the man's arm in one smooth movement, she twisted his wrist around to face his own chest and plunged the needle into him. The scream of pain he emitted was not registered by his attacker, for the sound of her heart pulsing in her ears blocked all else from entering.

Johnson was now lying motionless on the floor. Eva stood over him, eyes fixed upon the set of keys attached to his belt. She crouched by his side, her gaze darting briefly to his eyes. Confirming them to be shut and unflinching, she reached towards her ticket to freedom. As quickly as she grasped hold of them, a pair of cold, sweaty hands grabbed hold of her throat. She dropped the keys to the floor and began pulling at Johnson's wrists. Her attempts to break free proved to be in vain for his physical prowess greatly outweighed her frail and weakened body. With a struggle and a grunt of exertion, Johnson rolled Eva to the side and was now looming over her. The hands around her throat tightened as her large, blue eyes stared directly into his. Wild with rage, their vibrant greenness was shattered by growing threads of red.

Tears began to well. The pain pierced like bee stings. Such was the strength of Johnson's grip, any attempt Eva made to call out proved fruitless. Her ears began to ring. Her vision began to blur. A swift jab from her knee to his groin was enough to finally break his hold. Johnson reeled back in pain. Eva gasped, her lungs desperately trying to clutch at the air around her. Grabbing the syringe still protruding from her assailant's chest, she clenched her teeth and pulled it out. With another cry of pain, Johnson fell back, slamming against the ground. Scrambling for the keys, Eva stumbled to her feet.

Oblivious to the piercing cold of the concrete floor against her bare skin, she ran. Tresses of long, dark hair flowed behind her as one arm held in place the white, silken cloth that draped her pale body. The other arm, wrapped around her abdomen, supported the growing life within her bulging stomach.

Through the doorway and turning to her left, she refused to allow herself to hesitate. Pounding down the corridor she passed at least a dozen doors that undoubtedly led to rooms very much like the one from which she had just fled. How desperately she wished she could help the women concealed within but there simply was not enough time. Her one and only chance to save them all was to escape.

Tearing her way down the long path to freedom she reached the exit door at the far end - the location of which she had spotted and engrained in her mind long before. She looked to the keys, still tightly bundled together in one delicate hand. Her fingers released their grip, sending them cascading to the floor. Immediately she was crouching, searching her way through them for the one she needed; the one her life now so desperately depended on; for if one thing was still certain, it was that time was not on her side.

The sound of a wailing siren was enough to break through the tribal beating of her heart against her eardrums. At once the corridor was flooded with streams of revolving red lights that came from above. Time was indeed running out even faster than she had anticipated.

Her hands felt heavy as her vision began to blur again. Keys passed through her fingers clumsily in her now frantic search. Her eyes swivelled from the ground to the corridor and back again. When they next returned to the corridor, they were met with at least four men running towards her. She gasped.

Three failed to enter the lock as she made her way through the chain of keys as methodically as she could. A few more seconds were all that were required to find the right one. Sinking it into the padlock and twisting it to the left, the click that registered her success sent a shiver through her entire body.

Light poured in through the open door and burned her retinas to the point of temporary blindness. She stood motionless, like a startled doe, bathed in nothing but glorious warmth. Clarity returned and composure allowed her to pull the heavy, steel door closed behind her and secure the padlock in place. The sound of her pursuers pounding their fists against the barrier that now separated them soon faded away, replaced by delicate birdsong and the sweet smell of trees. She was free.

Chapter Two

Exhausted, Eva made her way through the dense woodland surrounding the complex. Crisp autumnal leaves brushed against her skin, while thick moss provided a soft, spongy pathway underfoot. In spite of all she had been through, she could not help but smile. In stark contrast to the dull greys and lifeless blacks that had engulfed her throughout the duration of her captivity, Eva's eyes were bombarded with luminous oranges, glowing yellows and fresh greens wherever she looked.

After around an hour's hurried walk and having made certain that the sirens had long been silenced, she felt she had established enough distance to allow herself a break. A fallen tree branch provided an ample seat upon which she could rest but her neck flinched from the sharp stinging in her mouth every time she tried to swallow. She needed water.

Upon stopping moving, the realisation of the extent of her situation hit home with a painful thud. Her chest audibly crackled with every quick breath; her lungs frenziedly trying to recuperate. Her feet were blistered and swollen, having taken the brunt of her fleeing. Her back throbbed deeply from the strain of Johnson's weight atop of her; the red marks left by his hands still wrapped around her throat. Pain pulsed through every inch of her small body. However, as her hand came to rest upon her stomach, all at once a sense of calm flowed through her veins and numbed her to all else she had been feeling. Kicking and wriggling, the innocence and obliviousness of the infant within her gave her the comfort she required. Her smile soon returned. She would allow herself only a few more minutes of this solace before deciding she must continue on her way.

When she lifted herself from the makeshift seat, her knees seized and she fell to the ground. Poised on all fours, she hoisted herself back to her feet and tentatively placed one foot in front of the other. She did not have any more time for pain; her pursuers would be well on their way to catching up with her by now and it was not safe to stay here.

The light of the sun gradually dimmed as the hours dwindled away, yet the colours of the forest seemed no less vibrant and alive. Eva's eyelids were heavy though, with every blink proving a struggle to lift them again. Every so often, golden-winged butterflies fluttered from the hedgerows and circled her or the call of a nearby bird rang out through the otherwise uninterrupted silence. Striking the perfect balance between beauty and irritancy, they kept her mind stimulated enough to provide the focus to stay awake for several more hours.

As she felt increasingly tired and unable to progress any further, her mind felt light and her vision hazy. The unwanted hands of dehydration had well and truly gripped her, as dangerous and life threatening as those of Johnson. Bending forwards and placing her hands on her knees for support, she sighed. Her movement through the undergrowth had evidently been making more noise than she had been aware of, as being still allowed her ears to be filled with a sound far sweeter than any bird; it was the sound of running water.

She threw her head up and turned from side to side like a lost lamb in search of its mother. She determined that the sound was coming from her left. Every inch of her being ached once again as she dragged her legs forward. Soon, she was using the weight of her body to push herself through a thick cluster of hedges. Stumbling out the other side, she came to a sudden halt. It was beautiful. The moon, now high above her head, glistened off the surface of the crystal clear pool that had formed at the bottom of the delicately trickling stream. Throwing herself forward and crashing to her knees again, Eva plunged her hands into the water, sending ripples cascading to the edges. Icy cold prickles pulsed through her body, making her feel more alive than she had in months. Her lips, dry as bone and heavily cracked, quivered as she scooped the water up to her face and began to drink. Clarity of mind returned, yet so did the reality of how physically and emotionally drained she now was.

She could not go any further tonight. Having walked for the majority of the day, the woodland was now almost entirely bathed in darkness. By this point, here was as safe a place as any to spend the night, so she shuffled round to the edge of the pool and sat with her back against a tree. Swinging her arms around, she pulled fallen leaves close to her body to form something as close to a blanket as she could before once again bringing her hands to a stop upon her stomach.

"Goodnight little guy."

Chapter Three

Her eyelids opened gradually, fluttering under the strain of the intense light bearing down on her. It took several minutes of staring up into the rich canopy above for the memories to return. Remembering where she was, Eva slowly sat up, the rustle of leaves a welcome change from the clink of rusted springs. Readjusting the thin material still draped across her body and securing the knot at the top which held it in place, she swivelled back round to the pool of water and drank again.

Rested and re-hydrated, she had no further reason to stay here and so was ready to leave. Men from the facility would no doubt have resumed their search for her this morning and she was unsure of just how long she had been asleep; therefore she knew it was wise to set off quickly. A clearer mind and a rested body meant however that the aches and pains had become far more prevalent. She did not know where she was going but knew she could not stop until she found help. Her only overarching plan was to somehow return to her parents and leave this nine month long nightmare in the past. The image of her ill and bedridden mother when last she had seen her was one that was too frightening to dwell on and was quickly brushed aside. The gut-wrenching loneliness; the nights she had lain awake picturing a reunion with her parents; the longing she felt to be held in their arms again; they could not have been for nothing.

Several hours later and the sharp jabs of thirst returned to her throat. Making her way into a small clearing, a sense of obscurity washed over her. Not a single leaf remained upon its tree here. Bare and sun-scorched branches reached out threateningly in all directions; their twigs like hands trying to grab hold of her. Knee-high in a pool of leaves as red as blood, Eva waded her way into the centre of the clearing and stood, absorbing her perplexing surroundings. There was nothing; no chirping of birds overhead; no rustle of leaves as a mouse scurried home; no trickle of water from a distant stream. In that moment, the world seemed to have stopped.

Life returned to this place in a way that made Eva's heart tremble. There, straight ahead, stood a man in black tactical clothing with a gun gripped tightly in his hands. The snap of a branch to the left jolted her head in search of its source. A second man was moving through the undergrowth no more than fifteen feet away from her. Frozen with fear, Eva did not dare to even so much as take a breath.

The man to her left was sweeping his way through the trees, scanning the ground for tracks, his prey far closer than he could anticipate, while the man to her front stood with his back to her, gun aimed out ahead of himself. There was nowhere to hide but if she ran, they would surely hear her. In this state of physical exhaustion, she was far from able to outrun them and so she stood, breathless and shaking; every muscle in her body tensed.

A few minutes of complete silence later, both men had moved away and were no longer in sight, yet Eva remained in this position for several moments longer. Somehow beyond her comprehension, she had managed to evade discovery. Rather than consider this encounter a lucky escape, she took it as a grave warning that confirmed her worst fears since her escape: Not only were they indeed looking for her but so very much worse than that, the weapons suggested with severity that they were not prepared to listen to reason.

When she finally felt the courage to breath openly, every gasp at the air felt like a kick in the chest. As the tension flowed from her body, she could feel her muscles gradually relaxing, one-by-one. A single, delicate tear charged its way down her porcelain skin. Turning to her right, she walked on.

Chapter Four

Walking for around two hours immersed Eva deep in the forest once again. Glorious birdsong returned and with it came new found optimism. Every step took her further from the facility and closer to civilisation and if the men she had encountered earlier had been the only search party pursuing her, then she was certain she was now heading in the opposite direction to them.

Eventually she came to another clearing in the trees. This one however was much larger with an old, dusty road running straight through the middle of it, leading off in either direction. With the thought that every road had to lead somewhere better than here, she had found her pathway out. Opting to continue heading in the direction that would take her furthest from her adversaries last known location and the facility from which they had come, she turned to her right without a second thought.

It was not long before the smile was wiped from her face as a figure came wandering out of the bushes on the left side of the path. It was a man and slung over his shoulder was a large, brown rifle. He stopped in his tracks and stared at her, eyes fixed like the sight of a sniper on their target. Eva stopped and stared too but not at him; at the weapon. A few seconds later without either of them having moved, a second figure emerged behind the man. Moving quickly, she placed her hands onto his back to steady herself.

"What is it?" the woman said, her voice husky and short of breath.

When she was met with no reply, she followed the direction of his gaze. Her eyes locked onto Eva as she let out a slight gasp.

"Who are you?" the man finally asked.

It was only then that Eva was able to shake her frozen state and inspect the situation more closely. This man, unlike those she had encountered before, was not wearing professional gear. His jeans were torn at the knees and his checked shirt with rolled sleeves was stained with dirt. She also quickly surmised that his weapon looked far less sophisticated than the ones they had carried. His companion was also evidently not one of her pursuers, as her red sweater did not make an ideal choice for sneaking through the trees undetected, nor did her distinct lack of any firearm make her properly equipped to apprehend an enemy. Most tellingly of all was the look of fear in their eyes and the wrinkled foreheads displaying the myriad of questions they undoubtedly had for her. No, these people had not been expecting to find her out here and the prospect of having help on her way sent Eva's pulse soaring.

"My name is Eva."

"What are you doing all the way out here, Eva?" said the man, his voice void of emotion.

"I escaped."

"Escaped? Escaped from where?" the woman asked, her head turned towards her partner.

"They call it 'Station 12'."

"And what exactly is 'Station 12'?" asked the man.

"A research facility." Eva's eyes moved down to face the ground. "Can you help me?" her head lifted to face them again almost immediately. "I need to get out of here. They're following me. Please, I just need to get back to my parents."

The man and woman looked at each other for a moment and the woman gave a brief nod.

"Come on." She gestured towards herself. "We'll take you into town."

"Thank you." said Eva, eyes closed and head

tilting backwards so the sunlight hit her face.

The couple began walking back in the direction from which they had come and Eva followed closely. A smile returned to her soft features and suddenly she did not care about the prickly pine needles digging into her bare and worn feet.

"So what are you guys doing all the way out here?" she asked.

"Hunting." said the man, his bluntness making Eva falter slightly.

"Our house, it's not too far from here. Around now is usually the best time to find some rabbit or a deer if you're really lucky." said the woman. "My name's…" she stopped mid-sentence when the man ground to an abrupt halt and turned towards her with a cold stare.

"My name is Delilah." she said, turning back to Eva. "And this is Thomas, my husband."

"Well thanks again for helping me." said Eva.

"We should keep moving." said Thomas, "It'll start getting dark soon."

"That's a good point." said Delilah, "It's too late to start heading to the city now. Our house is on the way anyway. We should just take her back to our place."

"No." said Thomas, glancing briefly towards Eva.

"Tom, look at her. She's exhausted and you've

always said yourself that it's safer to travel during the day."

Now it was Thomas who looked down to the ground. The three of them stood in silence, no one bold enough to be the first to look at any of the others.

"Thomas, please. We'll give her a roof for the night. Then we'll take her to the city first thing tomorrow."

Eva wrung her hands together nervously, still refusing to look up. She knew her ability to make it out of this forest could well depend on the outcome of this exchange, yet she felt entirely powerless to influence their decision.

"Fine." said Thomas, "But only for tonight."

"Of course." said Eva, "Thank you. Both of you."

Thomas immediately turned and continued walking, his rifle swinging erratically and jolting against his back with the sudden burst of movement. Feeling uncomfortable at her evident lack of welcome, Eva knew she had no choice but to follow, determining that it was a far better option than returning to wandering aimlessly through the woodland in the hopes of finding her own way into the nearest town.

As they walked Eva became more conscious of their circumstances and felt more sympathetic towards Thomas' hostile reaction. After all, it is not every day you stumble upon a heavily pregnant girl wrapped in a dirt clad sheet, mumbling about how she needs help to escape. She soon felt lucky that they were still willing to help at all; just being in her presence could be putting them in danger given the armed guards from 'Station 12' that were still in hot pursuit. That was a specific detail she felt it best not to reveal just yet.

The sun descended from the sky and disappeared behind a distant mountaintop, allowing darkness to weave its way through the tress once more. Just as the pain in her feet began to return, Eva heard the voice of Delilah calling from up ahead.

"We're here."

Breaking into a light jog that was as fast as her depleted physical state would allow, Eva soon caught up to her. There, nestled among the trees, was a small, stone-built cottage. Though it looked somewhat crumbled and dilapidated, the sight of decent shelter brought relief to Eva's heart.

"Home sweet home." said Delilah.

Chapter Five

The sights and smells overwhelmed Eva as she was led into the house. Her nostrils were assaulted by the scent of freshly made soup which sat in a large pot on the stove. Four chairs were tucked neatly under a large table in the middle of the kitchen while in the other half of the room, a sofa and two large, old armchairs formed a circle around a small radio on the centre of a round, wooden coffee table. Thomas placed his rifle in a glass cabinet against the wall and left the room by a door at the far end without looking back.

"Are you hungry?" Delilah's question was like music to Eva's ears.

"Yes." she replied, doing her best not to sound too desperate.

"I'll get you some soup. It's fresh. I just made it this morning." She opened a cupboard and brought out a bowl as she spoke. Heading over to the stove, she removed the lid and began ladling the contents generously into the bowl.

"It might have cooled down a little but we can't afford to light the stove again today I'm afraid. We're running low on matches you see." said Delilah.

"Oh don't worry. I'm sure it will still be lovely." Eva stared in awe at the large chunks of vegetables swimming in golden broth as they flowed into the bowl.

Delilah placed the feast on the table and gestured for Eva to sit.

"Thank you." Eva said while gazing down at the food. Her bump restricted her from pulling her chair close to the table but she leaned in and inhaled the steam rising from the soup. Closing her eyes, she basked for a moment in the sweet smells of carrot, potato and leek. Picking up the spoon that had been placed beside the bowl, she began to eat. Her taste buds sang as her mouth was met with its first proper meal in months but a few hurried mouthfuls later, Eva composed herself and paused to speak.

"It's delicious. Thanks again for everything."

Delilah did not respond. She had taken a seat at the opposite end of the table and was staring at Eva. She had a worried expression on her face and Eva realised this was the first time she had properly looked at her host. She estimated that Deilah was around forty years old but her furrowed brow and dark roots made her appear marginally older upon initial sight. Her hair looked dry and lifeless; her lips cracked and sore. Her clothes had evidently been worn a number of times before, their colours fading and tired.

Eva followed the line of Delilah's gaze. She realised she was looking at her stomach and Eva too began to feel uneasy.

"How many months pregnant are you?" Delilah asked finally, after a long and uncomfortable silence so deafening that it had made their ears begin to ring.

"About eight." Eva replied.

Delilah gave a brief nod but again said nothing.

"Do you and Thomas have any children?" Eva asked, adjusting herself in the chair.

"We did; two girls. They died during The Breakdown.

"I'm sorry." Eva's sympathy was genuine, for she also knew what it was to feel loss as a result of The Breakdown.

"You should finish your food, you look hungry." said Delilah, evidently feeling as perturbed by the conversation as Eva did. She rose slowly from her chair before continuing.

"I'll fetch you some clean clothes and you can go get cleaned up once you're done."

This time it was Eva who remained silent. She glanced up and gave a brief smile then returned to eating the soup in front of her.

Grateful to be able to return her focus to the food for a moment, Eva did all but lick the bowl but by the time she had scooped up the last remaining droplets of sweet broth, Delilah had already retuned.

"I'll show you to the bathroom." she said.

Eva stood and crossed the room as Delilah led her through the same door Thomas had used earlier. A small set of stairs led to the upper part of the house, where Eva assumed Thomas must now have been. Delilah instead pointed towards a door at the end of a small hallway by the bottom of the staircase.

"I've filled you a bucket of water and left you some clothes. Take your time."

"Thanks." Eva's feelings of unease began to leave her somewhat as she entered the bathroom and the door closed behind her with a click.

A bath, a toilet and a sink; that was all there was, save for a small mirror on one wall. The walls themselves were peeling and small strips of white paint lay discarded on the dusty floor. Peering into the bath, she saw a rusted bucket filled with water, an old rag of cloth bobbing at the top.

She untied the knot that held in place the draped material that covered her body. It floated delicately to the floor, settling around her ankles like a cloud.

Bending forwards slightly, she picked up the rag, squeezed it tightly and held it against the side of her face. It was cold but deeply refreshing.

Examining herself closely for the first time since her escape, the true extent of the brutality of the journey upon her body became undeniably clear. Cuts on her arms and legs oozed droplets of blood where branches had grazed her skin and bruises shined where she had taken a beating from the undergrowth. Her stomach, which seemed to have managed the ordeal relatively unscathed, swelled out in front of her and moved slightly as the child inside wriggled around. Tears began to well in her eyes again but not through fear or pain. This time, they came from happiness and genuine astonishment. She had done it: She was free.

Just a few minutes later and Eva was washed and dressed. Delilah had provided her with a pair of her khaki coloured jeans which fit snugly and a rather worn looking white shirt that presumably belonged to Thomas. She buttoned all but the top button and rolled the sleeves up to her elbows. In spite of her blossoming bump, the shirt was somewhat oversized but still felt more comfortable than the single silken cloth that had been her staple wardrobe for so long. Pulling on a pair of grey boots, she tried to ignore the searing pain emitting from her blistered heels.

Using a bobble also gifted to her by Delilah, she

scraped her hair back into a ponytail and looked into the mirror. Her bottom lip was burst and swollen on one side and a cut on her left eyebrow looked to her as though it would benefit from a few stitches. Hospitals were not exactly commonplace these days however and she knew full well that she would have to make do without and accept the future presence of the inevitable scar the wound would leave behind. Letting out a deep sigh, she left the bathroom and headed back towards the kitchen.

She entered to find Delilah and Thomas sitting next to each other at the table. Eva's dishes had been cleared away and both of her hosts turned to watch her as she made her way into the room.

"Come and sit." said Thomas; his voice as lacking in feeling as it was earlier. His words felt less like an offer and more a command, so Eva did as he said.

Once sitting, she looked across the table, first at Delilah, then at Thomas.

"So," he said, "I think it's about time you told us who you are."

Chapter Six

Eva Cole had been a relatively normal girl with a relatively normal life. That was, until The Breakdown. This was the name given to the four year period when food and medical supplies fell so low that society began to turn upon itself. Abrupt and unforeseen changes in climate had allowed the development of tropical diseases to spread like a plague across the entire globe. Death and destruction became a way of life and anarchy and chaos soon followed as a result. When the streets were overwhelmed with riots, thousands more were killed, including Eva's own older brother, Tristan.

Importing and exporting shut down with every country opting to desperately cling on to whatever few resources they had left, while immigration was forbidden through fear of further exposure to new viruses. Crops were ruined and bodies were soon ravished by illness and hunger. Thus, paranoia became more common than conception and the world was slowly dying.

In what survived of America, strict control was exacted upon the everyday lives of its few remaining citizens and Eva had become a victim in the frantic Government's latest misguided efforts to repopulate its sparse States.

When it became apparent that one of the adverse effects of the spreading disease was a rapid fall in fertility rates, panic truly set in. Coupled with a fear of intimacy, general malnutrition and poor health overall, birth rates plummeted around the world, while growing protest against Governmental control led to a parallel increase in the rate of death as a direct result of rioting. Humanity was destroying itself. Rationing of food and medicine could not stop it; the ban on immigration could not stop it. Every contingency plan failed. Even though The Breakdown was declared officially over on September 28th 2041 following no new reported cases of disease for six months, the Earth seemed damaged beyond repair. Entire cities had been razed to the ground with nature slowly reclaiming the land.

Eva, along with her parents, had survived in the aftermath of the decaying world for a further two years as the population continued to slowly die out. Then, over eight months ago, now nineteen years old, she and sixty-four other women between the ages of eighteen and thirty were selected to be part of the American Government's latest endeavour to try and save what remained of civilisation.

All sixty-five women received the same letter; an invitation to discuss a governmental proposal of global importance. Upon attendance at this meeting, presented by three of the seven remaining US government officials at City Hall in what was once Los Angeles, now the hub of the vast majority of survivors, it soon became apparent that fertility and population were the topics of concern. They explained that the situation was now so critical that they deemed artificial insemination of young women the only viable option to begin the long and difficult process of repopulating the world and that these women, selected from the previous year's emergency census, had been chosen as the first batch of candidates to trial the programme.

Compliance was compulsory. Seized and sedated, the women were transported to 'Station 12', where they were impregnated and isolated from the frail remains of society. Fearing forced abortions and miscarriages, they were held in solitary confinement until the birth of their babies, upon which the infants would be taken to be placed under governmental care.

Eva had escaped precisely eight months and two

days after she was impregnated. A day later she was found by Thomas and Delilah and now, she sat across from them at their kitchen table, staring at the blank expressions upon their faces as she retold the previous events of her life.

Chapter Seven

When she was finished, Eva tilted her head downwards, preferring not to look at her audience. Her hands, warm and sticky with nerves, were wringing together under the table out of sight. No one spoke for several minutes. Though she could not yet bring herself to look directly at them again, Eva was aware that Delilah and Thomas were staring at one another, each most likely hoping that the other would make the first move.

"We'll take you into the nearest town first thing tomorrow." Thomas said, his deep voice like a gong breaking through the silence.

With that, he rose from his chair and began heading for the door again. Delilah silently lifted an outstretched hand towards him. His back already turned, he did not notice. Just Eva and Delilah remained and the eerie silence weaved its way through the room once more, its icy grip firmly upon the occupiers.

"You must be tired." Delilah spoke but just as Eva had done earlier, refused to look at the recipient of her words.

"A little." Eva lied, for her mind was far too active for her to be able to feel tired. Questions forced their way in and whirled around, each one vying for the utmost attention.

"You can sleep on the sofa. It's old but still comfortable enough." said Delilah.

"Thank you."

Without once allowing her gaze to meet Eva's, Delilah swept across the room and lifted the neatly folded blanket that lay along the back of the sofa. In one confident movement, she gripped an end tightly and threw her arms up in the air. The blanket unfolded mid-flight and dust particles were sent cascading across the room, dancing through the air in search of a new surface upon which to rest before the blanket delicately settled across the sofa.

"I'll see you in the morning." said Delilah, her voice now so soft it was barely audible.

"Good night." Eva replied. She tried to make eye contact to display her gratitude but just as her husband had done before her, Delilah turned her back and was heading for the door. Without any further exchanges, she left the room, pulling the door closed behind her. The sound of her footsteps upon the creaking staircase echoed out into the night and when the silence returned, Eva sighed.

Knowing she would not yet sleep if she tried, Eva glanced around the room, surveying its details fully instead. The furniture was basic, as was the norm of all households since The Breakdown. The absence of a television or phone would at one time have seemed absurd but not in this world. Cobwebs clung to the ceiling, yet cleaning was hardly a priority for the modern homemaker. The flames of the candles illuminating the room flickered. Shadows loomed to and fro upon the pale walls and Eva was reminded of the place that had served as her prison for so long.

Her heart rate rising as the painful memories began to creep their way in, she stood and moved away from the table. Finding herself staring at Thomas' rifle, proudly displayed in its glass cabinet, Eva paused. The red shoulder strap bore its owner's name in golden embroidery: *Thomas Cain.* The gun and cabinet themselves were two of the very few items contained within the room not coated in a murky layer of dust; evidently they were used on a regular basis. Reminding her of the armed men she had encountered in the woodland, Eva turned away again. This time, she was met with the sight of the window on the far wall.

She walked and stood before it. The outside world felt somewhat threatening now. A cold wind whistled through the forest; an owl screeched in the distance. Trees swayed, their branches creaking under the pressure of the breeze. The snap of a twig underfoot from an unseen animal punctured the air. The moon, almost full and high above the landscape, cast its light unevenly upon the scene; lacing in and out of the trees, revealing some sights and hiding others.

Finding she could look no longer, Eva turned and made for the sofa, opting not to extinguish the candles. Wrapping the blanket around herself tightly, she formed a hand knitted, dark red cocoon of protection against her fears. Lying down, she used the solitary cushion as a pillow upon which to rest her head.

Barely blinking and certainly not sleeping, Eva waited while the hours slowly dwindled away, the faces of her mother and father floating in and out of her mind intermittently. The candle light had long since burned out by the time the moon retreated behind the hills as the sun rose triumphantly to ignite the world with life once more. Rays of light beamed in through the formerly frightening window and so darkness loosened its grasp and faded away. Heart rate eased and fear receding, Eva felt victorious over the night.

Chapter Eight

Delilah appeared first. Dressed in a pale blue knitted jumper that was punctured with small holes and faded black jeans that were frayed at the hem, she spoke few words to her guest before heading outside to fetch eggs and milk for breakfast. Residing in a small wooden barn behind the house were three dilapidated hens, their feathers sparse and tired looking. They were joined by a solitary goat, its eyes full of sorrow; its coat grey and matted.

The trio sat around the table eating a small portion of oats drizzled with a few drops of milk obtained from the goat. Having found that the hens had failed to produce any eggs, they had to be foregone.

Struggling yet again to make any solid eye contact with her hosts and with conversation virtually non-existent, the atmosphere over breakfast felt so dense it was almost tangible. Minutes passed with no sound besides the gentle clinking of spoons against bowls as they busied themselves with eating their food.

"Thank you Delilah." Eva had pushed the remaining debris from the oats around her bowl for as long as she felt she could. She placed the spoon inside it and slid the bowl towards the centre of the table before leaning back in her chair and resting her hands upon her stomach.

"You're welcome." said Delilah, immediately rising and gathering the dishes. Evidently she and Thomas had also been finished for some time and had shared in Eva's awkwardness; once again waiting for her to act first as she had hoped they would. She crossed the room and began placing the bowls and spoons into the sink one by one, drawing out the duration of the task to a length far longer than required.

"We should leave now." said Thomas, "It's quite a journey to get into town." Eva jumped slightly in her chair as his voice abruptly shattered the silence. This was the first time he had spoken all morning.

"We'd better take the truck." said Delilah, turning her head to look at her husband as she spoke.

"You're right." he replied, "It'll be safer."

Despite her obvious presence, Eva felt distinctly left out of the conversation. She looked from

Thomas to Delilah and back again but just as had been the case on the previous evening; neither would meet her gaze no matter how much she persisted in trying.

"I'll just fetch my coat and we'll go." said Delilah, a sense of haste to her voice.

"Good." said Thomas, "Let's get this done."

He rose from his chair and moved to the glass cabinet. Opening its door, he lifted his gun out carefully and slung it over his shoulder. As he did this, Delilah hurried from the room, her footsteps clattering like thunder as she ran up the stairs. Thomas continued to make no attempt to speak or even look at Eva while his wife was absent. A moment later, she noisily made her way back down the stairs and reentered the room, this time wearing a thick coat made from an indistinguishable but undeniable animal skin of sorts. Such luxuries were rare now and Eva had no doubt that Thomas must have been the one to kill and skin the beast used to produce this spectacle. The sight made Eva wrinkle her nose slightly for she had never approved of cruelty towards animals and always maintained that had it not been for the scarcity of food, she would have forgone meat in her diet altogether.

"Ready?" Delilah asked, again aiming her words at Thomas rather than Eva.

"Let's go." he replied.

With that, husband and wife made for the door. With no invitation or recognition of any kind, for a brief moment, Eva hesitated as to whether they even intended for her to follow but with the door left open in their wake and little other choice, she felt it best to simply do so anyway.

Standing in the doorway, she gave the interior of the house one last look before following the couple outside. Blood red, a sheer monster of metal; the truck loomed before her. Thomas was already sitting in the driver's seat as Delilah was climbing into the passenger's side. Eva moved to the door behind where Delilah now sat and began clambering in. The height of the truck from the ground due to its thick tyres combined with Eva's bulging stomach made this endeavour a tricky one but after a few sighs and an exertion of effort, she was in and the door was pulled firmly shut behind her with a bang.

A roar and a jolt erupted from the machine as the engine came to life. A cloud of dark smoke shot out from the exhaust like a bullet and dispersed into the air, swirling around the vehicle and lashing at the windows. Eva pulled the seatbelt over her and clicked it into place. After a hurried backwards U-turn and a bumpy escape from the tarnished driveway, they were on the road, the house soon disappearing from sight.

"How long does it take to get to town from

here?" asked Eva.

"A couple of hours." said Thomas. His hands were gripping the steering wheel so tightly that his knuckles drained of colour. His rifle rested between the front seats by the gear stick so as to remain easily within his grasp at all times.

Eva glanced at the rearview mirror and found Delilah's eyes looking directly into hers. In an instant, Delilah averted her gaze. Eva now felt more than a little wary.

After about twenty minutes of driving without a further word being spoken and with tensions now simmering towards boiling point, sights flitting past the windows began to look familiar. They soon passed a clearing in the trees with a dirt path in between; the place Eva was certain was the spot which had played host to her first meeting with the couple sitting silently before her.

"Where are we going?" she asked, struggling to keep her voice steady through the nerves swelling in her heart.

"We're taking you into town." said Thomas.

Sunlight flooded in through the windows and glistened off the golden thread on the strap of the gun, making Thomas' name stand out against its deep red backdrop. The weapon's mere presence was starting to scare Eva, the sound of her own heartbeat returning to her ears as blood pulsed to her face and flushed her pale skin.

"You said last night your house was on the way into town." Eva spoke as clearly as she could. She was not asking a question nor was she in any doubt, for she was certain of Delilah's claim; her words from the previous evening now circling through her mind.

"It is." said Thomas.

"Then why are we going back the way we came?"

Upon her question, Thomas' foot slammed against the break and the truck violently lurched to a halt. They all strained themselves against the momentum of the vehicle's prior speed before slumping back in their seats. Delilah continued to stare forward as Thomas turned his head to look straight at Eva for the first time all day.

"You're not taking me into town, are you?" Eva's voice quivered, unable to stop the fear from penetrating any longer. When a reply did not come, she continued, almost certain of the situation she now faced but determined to confirm the truth.

"When I told you I escaped from a facility, why didn't you ask me about it? You haven't asked me a single thing about what happened to me there."

She did not expect to receive a response and sure enough, none came. Eva's final words hit her as strongly as they did the others.

"You knew."

She pressed the button to release the seatbelt, the click that signaled its freedom finally attracting the gaze of Delilah.

"Don't." said Thomas. His hand was gripping the gun.

Eva stared into Thomas' eyes. Violent and bloodshot, they reminded her of Johnson's. With no further motivation required, she threw open the door and jumped from the truck. She stumbled as her boots sank into dense marsh-like mud. With every ounce of effort she could muster, she ran. Off the road and into the trees, she did not dare look back but the sound of slamming doors and panicked shouts confirmed that the Cain's were in pursuit.

Random gunshots began ringing out into the air, the sound of bullets as they whistled past her causing Eva to flinch but not to slow down.

Birds squawked and fled from their nests in the sudden commotion assaulting the otherwise tranquil scene. Twigs snapped, leaves rustled and branches scratched as Eva pushed her way through the thick woodland. The shouts grew more frequent as the gunshots grew sparser but Eva continued to run.

A few minutes later, she finally stopped. Glancing around, her efforts to determine any form of bearings or plan failed; the sense of panic still all consuming. Her feet pulsed as her blisters bled from the friction of the boots. Her chest heaved as her lungs cried out for air. Thomas' voice returned in the distance.

Just as the pressure began to overwhelm her and she froze in desperation, the baby kicked. For a second, all else disappeared and Eva found salvation in her own private world. There was no fear, no panic and no danger; just mother and child alone. Her sweaty, shaking hands pressed against the source of the kick and a smile illuminated her face.

With this reassurance that she was not alone and the determination of having another life to protect besides her own, Eva was able to run once more but she knew her pursuers had been granted time to close in on her location and she could not outrun them for much longer in her current condition. Now more focused in her escape, she spotted a thick patch of shrubbery with a small opening at the bottom. Deciding her best option was to conceal herself inside it; she fell to her knees and began forcing her arms in. Thorns pierced her skin and tore at her shirt but the adrenaline now coursing through her system left her oblivious to the pain. Once inside the undergrowth, she waited.

One hand clasped her mouth to quell her gasps for breath while the other cradled her stomach and the infant residing within. Footsteps grew louder as the hunters moved closer. Delilah came into sight, moving through the trees and scanning the area around her. With one of her enemies now standing no more than ten feet away, Eva's foot slipped and the snap of a branch rang out, as loud to Eva's heart as the gunshots had been to her ears.

Delilah whipped her head around and strained her eyes, leaning forwards towards the hedgerow. For a moment, Eva was sure that she had been discovered but her attention being stolen by something in the distance, Delilah quickly moved on.

Removing her hand from her mouth, every muscle in Eva's body seemed to relax at once. Tension flowed from her limbs as deep gulps at the air replenished her lungs. At least an hour passed before the sun began to fade away and the icy grip of darkness returned to the world again. Having neither seen nor heard any further sign of her would-be betrayers, Eva crawled out of her hiding place and got to her feet, legs quivering like those of a new born deer from the strain they had once again been forced to endure.

"They knew." Eva said aloud. Her voice met only with the screech of an owl and the whistle of the wind. "They knew."

Chapter Nine

Eva surmised that the already dire situation that had befallen society had worsened even more so during her captivity and was no longer under any illusions as to just how dangerous the world could be. Now certain that the seemingly oblivious Cain family had already been very much aware of 'Station 12' and precisely what had been happening behind those walls, she realised they had been intending to take her back to her former prison all along. Perhaps they even worked there. Having at first seemed a helpful, if somewhat reserved couple, Eva now felt utterly betrayed and foolish for ever having trusted them. She was determined that if nothing else, she would never make the same mistake again.

Once more, she found herself wandering in the depths of the flourishing forest and with little clue as to her location, all she could do was walk in the opposite direction that Delilah had taken. The previous pristine whiteness of her shirt was now tarnished by flecks of ruby red where trees had clawed at her skin and thorns had torn their way into her flesh. Her feet ached with every step and had it not been for her inability to safely determine the condition of the ground underfoot now concealed by darkness, she would have removed her boots to relieve the pressure upon the blisters that flaked her heels.

Having been so desperate to find other survivors during her last solitary trip through woodland territory, it was remarkable how much Eva's attitude had changed in a matter of mere hours. Now she desired solitude; to avoid roads and pathways and silently weave her way through the trees like a shadow, staying as hidden from view as she possibly could. The only people she hoped to see now were her mother and father, whom she missed more than ever, despite having been apart from them since the day before her abduction.

One thing was still very much the same as the last time however; she needed to find a source of water. Her throat as dry as sand, the pain each time she swallowed felt like the thorns were now scratching her from the inside, her eyes clenching shut and head twisting to the side each time to push past the discomfort. Stopping only occasionally to rest against the trunk of a tree or to sit on a discarded branch, she continued on her journey as much as her body would allow in spite of the limited visibility.

Though without aid in her mission once again and armed with a far less discernible route to follow, Eva's intentions remained the same as they had been when accompanied by Thomas and Delilah. She had to find a way into the nearest town so as to somehow reunite with her family. Her betrayal had granted her an even greater understanding of the extent of the measures the American people would now take to fight against their fear of others, to obey what frailties remained of governmental control and to strive to support the repopulation of their dying country. More clear in her mind was her aim and more determined than ever before was she to see it come to fruition; Eva knew she had to expose the truth.

Chapter Ten

Beams of light punctured the night and pushed the darkness into submission as the sun rose over the far-off hilltops. The owls were silenced and the bats retreated to their covens as birdsong returned to the air and flowers opened in welcome of a new day. Unlike the days prior however, dull clouds loomed over much of the land, restricting the full glory of the sun from being known. An unwelcome chill found its way into the normally refreshing breeze and Eva walked with her arms folded across her chest in an attempt to retain what little warmth there was.

In mid-afternoon, just as the familiar pang of her blistered heels began to kick in once again, a single drop of water struck the top of Eva's head. She stopped and listened. The gentle patter of stray droplets soon swelled into the glorious hiss of rainfall. Cleansing her of both dirt and blood, Eva raised her arms to shoulder height and stretched them out as far as they would go. Tilting her head back, she allowed the water to flow down the soft features of her face, now complete with smile.

Realising the other opportunity this shower provided, Eva began to look around for the biggest leaves she could find. Opting for those that hung from what she believed to be a paulownia tree – a fact she had picked up from her mother's vast knowledge of natural life – she placed her hands delicately on either side of a single, large leaf, taking care not to tear it. Curving the edges upwards, she shaped the still attached leaf into a sort of funnel and tilted it down towards her face; her mouth open wide like an eager chick, waiting to collect the fresh water gathering within the makeshift receptacle.

The rate of the rainfall was so that it replenished the small pool of water even as she drank. Twenty seconds or so of solid gulps and Eva released the leaf from her delicate touch with a satisfied sigh. A sense of reprieve washed over her as easily and fluidly as the rain itself and immediately her situation felt more manageable.

Unsure at first exactly why the sound of the rain continued to raise such feelings of excitement and intrigue even after its purpose of both shower and water source had been fulfilled, it soon dawned that she had neither seen nor heard rain during the entire time of her confinement. A new appreciation for the wonders of nature was instilled within her very being and despite the succession of ordeals that had become her very way of life, the smile spread across her face failed to leave her for several minutes.

When at last the bombardment of rain began to recede and the sound of trickling water was replaced once again by the hustle and bustle of life within the woodland, Eva decided now was as good a time as any to allow herself another brief rest. Stopping before the nearest tree, she turned, leaned her back against it and used her hands to slide down until she sat upon the ground. Rays of sunshine now at full power, the grey clouds soon dispersed and Eva was basked in all-encompassing warmth, the remains of the water on her skin fading away and returning to the air. Her head soon began to lull as her eyelids fluttered; lashes brushing softly like the delicate feathers of a dove. By soundtrack of chirping finches, she drifted off to sleep.

Chapter Eleven

With a jolt and a sharp intake of breath, Eva woke from her slumber. Blurred vision and momentary confusion as to where she was soon lifted as her eyes refocused the scene before her. Having only intended to rest her feet for a few minutes, Eva was annoyed at having allowed herself to fall asleep. With an undeterminable journey ahead of her, she knew she needed to utilise the daylight hours as fully as possible and only rest properly under cover of night. With a grunt produced equally from physical exertion as it was frustration, she used the trunk of the tree upon which she had leaned to pull herself up.

Darkness had not yet plagued the land, providing some reassurance that not too much potential travel time had dwindled away while she had slept but the sudden effort that seemed necessary to support the weight of her body and the tiny crystals that had gathered in the corner of each eye suggested the impromptu nap had lasted longer than she would like to hope.

Something odd struck her as she stood, hands still clasped to the tree. Despite the last remaining surge of light still being emitted from the sun, her surroundings seemed unusually quiet again. The once glorious chorus of life had been hushed; the whistle of the wind on hold. Crisp leaves lay motionless on the ground, their rustle contained within. With memories of the last time such silence had befallen the forest, Eva's heart rate began to rise again. She stood, fixed to the spot, her grip on the tree tightening with each passing second. Sharp protrusions of bark pressed tightly against the palms of her hands but she dared not to move even enough to distinguish the pressure.

Time seemed to slow when a man emerged from behind a cluster of trees to her left. Wearing all too familiar black tactical gear and brandishing a rifle, he moved without a sound, like a panther stalking its prey. A lump swelled in Eva's throat; her eyes began to sting. She could feel the blood within her body rushing towards her head, flushing her face and leaving her hands cold and tingling.

Still holding on, she edged around to the other side of the tree to try and conceal herself. Then, at once, she knew the likely cause of this latest threat:

Thomas and Delilah Cain. The convenience of their sudden reappearance seemed too obvious to ignore; they must have alerted the security at 'Station 12' as to her whereabouts. She moved in closer and pressed herself against the tree as tightly as her stomach would allow. Shutting her eyes for a few seconds and taking a single, slow breath – in through the nose and out through the mouth – she readied herself for another potential pursuit. She began to peer out from behind her shield. Eyes now wide and lips pursed, the view ahead gradually revealed itself. Before her hunter had even been fully exposed, a shot tore through the air. With a sharp scream, Eva whipped her head back into cover. Shards of bark sprayed out as the bullet grazed the side of the tree where Eva's face had been not a moment before.

Adrenaline kicked in as it so often had to in Eva's recent life. Without even the time to consider a course of action, she turned and she ran. The chase commenced immediately. There was no pain from bursting blisters or exhausted lungs this time however, as fear overwhelmed every inch of her body and threw her senses into overdrive. Thunderous footsteps from behind grew ever louder. Her arms pounded at the air, her entire body working in unison to propel her forwards as quickly as it could.

A searing pulse of pain struck her left calf and

immediately she knew she had been shot. Tumbling forwards, her arms thrusting out to try and break the fall, she slammed into the ground. Dust and leaves briefly formed a cloud around her, the force of the landing cascading them into the air before they settled on the ground once more.

Tears poured down her face, mingling with the dirt now smeared there. Sliding onto her side, she turned her head and pulled her leg in towards herself. Jeans now torn and ragged, her white skin was tarnished by a stream of red as blood flowed from the open wound; the bullet still wedged inside. Eva tried to cry out but no sound came. Rolling onto her back and propping herself onto her elbows, she willed herself to use any pitiful reserves of energy remaining to try and drag herself to safety.

The man stepped up before her, blocking all else from view. They stared into each other's eyes; hers wide and pleading, his cold and merciless. He raised his gun and pointed it towards her chest. Finger poised on the trigger, he prepared to finish his mission.

Just as the trigger was pulled, he reeled back and the bullet missed its target. A rock had pummeled his shoulder and thrown him off balance.

"Son of a bitch!" he yelled, eyes darting around wildly like an enraged animal.

Another rock flew out of the trees from an

unseen saviour, this one striking the soldier's face. Dropping his weapon to the ground, he threw his hands up and clasped them over his right eye while stumbling backwards and writhing in pain. Barely able to move, Eva remained on her back. A cluster of hurried footsteps sounded before a set of warm hands took hold of her shoulders. Having been raised into a sitting position, her arm was hoisted around someone's shoulders and she was lifted to her feet.

Drifting in and out of consciousness, Eva knew she was being led away by her protector but had no idea where to or even who this mysterious hero was. A gentle voice was whispering to her and though she could not determine what it was saying, the soft, warm tone was strangely comforting through the pain and confusion.

Stopping before what appeared in her blurred vision to be merely a mass of leaves and vines; a hand reached out and disappeared into the foliage. A door opened as the greenery pulled back to reveal the entrance to some sort of hut. Plunging into darkness, they entered the hideaway. Eva was placed on a bed, her head lowered gently onto a welcoming pillow.

The hazy silhouette of a man stood before her but before she could discern any features or offer any word of thanks, her mind and body succumbed to their assault.

Chapter Twelve

Interrupted only by the occasional sound of a muted whisper or the brief flash of light let in by the flutter of her eyelids, Eva's senses were engulfed by darkness. Numb to her pain and motionless in spite of her effort, she lay, waiting for clarity and freedom of movement to return. Held captive within a useless frame, her mind was still very much active as questions and fears bombarded her brain. Who had saved her? Why had they risked their own life to do so? How long had she been lying here? Had her mysterious saviour worked alone or did he have accomplices? Was it some sort of trap? Could she really trust them? A mixture of excitement and apprehension gripped her in anticipation of finding answers to these and many other questions.

Her hearing was the first of her senses to return to its former glory. Birds could be heard chirping outside, though their delicate, faded tones implied that the structure within which she resided was fairly substantial. Evidently not alone, the general bustle of another inhabitant moving around could be heard clearly. The lack of any communication suggested that perhaps her rescuer had worked alone after all; a realisation that initially saddened Eva but on closer consideration, her earlier encounter with Thomas and Delilah had proven that in this world, safety in numbers was not always necessarily the case.

When finally she mustered the strength to prise open her eyes for more than a second, she strained to bring them back into focus. As they did so, a figure gradually appeared before her. Sitting on the other side of the small room was not the chiselled warrior she had expected to find but a rather scrawny looking boy. Perhaps her hero had a son?

Their eyes had met but neither had spoken; Eva through lack of ability and the young boy through his obvious and visible nerves. Sitting on a hand-woven, wicker chair, his knees were pulled up to his chest with his feet resting on the seat. He was clutching some sort of oily rag, wringing it tightly in his hands, all the while biting on his bottom lip.

Eva attempted to introduce herself but the resulting failure to produce any words made her cough, her chest crackling. Coughing again to try and clear the lump in her throat caused a sharp pain to shoot up into her head but finally granted the much desired access to speech.

"I'm Eva." she said. Her voice was hoarse and her chest now wheezed as she spoke. When her present company did not reply, she attempted further to draw out a response.

"What's your name?" she asked.

"I'm... I'm Matthew."

"How old are you, Matthew?"

"Twelve."

"I'm nineteen."

She tried to prop herself onto her elbows and sit up to get a closer look at her surroundings but an agonising sting shot up her leg and she was quickly reminded of her injury. With a grimace, she lay back on the pillow in defeat.

"Where are we?" she asked.

"It's my house now." said Matthew, eyes darting to the ground.

"Do your parents live here too?"

"No."

"Oh, I'm sorry." said Eva, her voice lowering. She did not need to ask what had happened to them. It was written all over the boy's face that his parents were long since dead.

"Do you live here alone?" Eva asked, hoping for both of their sakes that perhaps he had an older sibling or at least a kindly guardian.

"Yes." His response was muffled as he clenched the rag tighter.

Eva also looked down to the ground now. Another casualty of the cruelties of The Breakdown, her heart swelled in sympathy for the child sitting before her. She wrestled with herself, for her mind was abound with questions but she remained reluctant to push on such a sensitive subject with a child so evidently affected by the harsh world they now lived in.

"How long was I asleep?" she asked, deciding it best to change the topic of conversation.

"Nearly a day I think."

"Wow. I guess I was tired." She smiled slightly and raised her eyebrows as she spoke, hoping to lighten the tense atmosphere surrounding them and put the boy at ease. He did not look up to meet her gaze but she saw a faint smile spread across his innocent features.

"So…" she poised herself to ask the real question that burned in her brain, "Was it you who saved me?"

"Yeah."

"Thank you." Eva's response was heartfelt, though she was still amazed that her heroic saviour was so young.

"You're welcome." This time he did look up. The sincerity and warmth in both his answer and his face moved Eva. She could feel tears making their way into her eyes but she struggled to keep them at bay, not wanting her new host to feel any more uncomfortable.

Fighting against the pain, she pushed herself up until she sat and slid back so she could rest against the wall behind the pillow. Her face scowled and she grunted as she did so; her leg had clearly been hurt badly. Pulling the blanket back she braced herself for the horrific sight of a fresh, bloodied wound. Instead she found that her jeans had been neatly cut off from the knee to expose the lower half of her left leg, the entirety of which was wrapped in an immaculate looking white bandage that was held in place with a gold coloured safety pin.

"You did this too?" she looked back to Matthew as she spoke, the disbelief clear in her voice.

"Yeah."

Eva looked back down at her dressed leg and gently placed both hands on the bandages. A smile returned to her face and without looking back up, she spoke again.

"Where did you learn to do this?"

"My mum used to be a nurse." said Matthew. His answer was met initially with a silence while Eva carefully selected her words before responding.

"She taught you well. Thanks Matthew."

Tearing her gaze away from the wondrous

handiwork of her young hero, Eva scanned the room, taking in her new surroundings at last. It was some sort of cabin; built from sturdy looking wooden boards. There were no windows; the light coming instead from a lantern which rested on a small table in the far right corner, opposite the bed upon which she lay, while a few small candles scattered around provided some additional visibility. On the left, a small pile of kitchen utensils including pots and pans sat upon a larger table with a wash basin.

Almost in unison with her eyes meeting the pans, Matthew's quiet voice spoke out; the first time he had done so unprovoked.

"Are you hungry?"

"A little." answered Eva.

"I can't really cook but I've got some fresh vegetables if you want."

"Where did you get those?"

"My dad set up a garden out back when we came here. He wanted us to be able to mostly keep to ourselves."

"You've done enough. I don't want to take your food as well."

"It's okay. There's still plenty. I've kept them growing since…" he tailed off towards the end of his sentence. He got to his feet and went over to the table. Reaching into the basin, he pulled out two freshly washed and peeled carrots. He handed one to

Eva before sitting back in his chair.

The crunch was so satisfying as Eva bit into the raw carrot; the sweet, fresh flavour a welcome distraction from the pain that swirled around her entire body. As she took another bite, she glanced over at Matthew. Clutching the carrot in both hands, he ate his quickly, shovelling in bite after bite before he even had time to swallow the previous one. His mouth stuffed full and only a small piece left in his hands, he looked up and smiled; his puffed out cheeks struggling to contain the mouthfuls of carrot as he strained to stifle his laughter.

With a soft giggle, Eva could feel herself relaxing. Looking over at Matthew, she knew. She could see it in his face; she could see it in his eyes; she could trust him.

Chapter Thirteen

For the next five days, the new companions followed the same routine: They would eat a quick breakfast of dried oat biscuits before Matthew would head out for a few hours to tend to the vegetable garden and gather some water. Upon his return, he would be brandishing four carrots – two for each of them – and on one day he also had a few newly ready potatoes which he boiled in water over a small fire just outside the cabin. While Matthew was busy, Eva would rest on the bed, reading books lent to her by her gracious host. She made it through an average of two a day; some she had heard of before and some she had not.

Each morning, as he was leaving, Matthew would carefully scour the surrounding area to check for any threat. Once he had determined that the coast was clear, he would return to open the door to the cabin to allow fresh air and sunlight to flood the interior while he was gone. Once Matthew had finished his daily horticulture and dinner of fresh vegetables or berries had been eaten, the two would sit by candle light and talk of life before The Breakdown: their families, their schools, their friends and their hobbies; all of which had now been taken from them. Eva had far more to tell; Matthew having been too young to remember much of life before the world collapsed but he seemed content enough to simply listen and wonder.

One topic of conversation that never arose however was why Eva had been fleeing from an armed security official in the middle of the forest. By the third evening, Eva also realised that Matthew had never really enquired about her pregnancy beyond asking how many months along she was and if she knew the infants gender; the answer to the latter being that she did not. By the evening of the fifth day, she decided to raise the issue herself and so once normal conversation had dwindled away, they had finished marvelling at the bullet Matthew had removed from Eva's leg and a few moments of comfortable silence had befallen the room, she picked her moment to speak.

"Matthew, why have you not asked about the man who was chasing me?"

"I figured you wouldn't want to talk about it." he

said. His clear, emerald green eyes looking directly into hers confirmed the truth in his words.

"Do you know who he was?" she asked.

"He had a gun and a uniform so I guess he was from one of the Stations."

"Yeah, he was."

Their eye contact was lost when Matthew looked over at the lantern burning brightly in the corner of the room.

"Do you know which Station he was from?" asked Eva.

"Twelve is the closest."

"How many are there?"

"I don't know. I've heard people mention 'Station 14' though, so there's at least that many." Matthew answered without faltering but continued to look at the lantern.

"Do you know what happens at the stations?" Eva asked; her voice unbroken by even a hint of hesitation. She trusted him enough by now to be so bold.

"Experiments. Research. Stuff like that."

"Do you know what they research at 'Station 12'?"

"Pregnancy." he said. His eyes returned to meet hers as he did so.

His answer sent a shiver down Eva's spine. First Thomas and Delilah knew and now even Matthew.

Did the whole world know what was happening in 'Station 12'? Was there even a truth to expose; or did everyone already know and were simply choosing to ignore it?

"Yeah." she said, swallowing away the lump in her throat and regaining her composure as best she could. "I was there but I got away. Security guards have been chasing me ever since. I met up with a couple of people but they tried to take me back. Then you found me." The events replayed in her mind as she spoke, the enormity of her situation sinking further in and the longing to return home and leave this nightmarish life behind her overwhelming.

"What are you going to do?" he asked; his voice full of awe. Clearly this was information he had been curious about ever since their first encounter.

"I was trying to make it into the nearest town so I can get back to my parents but I have no idea where to go. I don't even know where we are."

"You could use the truck." said Matthew; an excited smile dominating his face as he spoke.

"What truck?"

"There's a truck that runs back and forward from the city. It brings medicine for us and we give them food to take back. You could use it."

"That's perfect." said Eva, she too becoming increasingly animated by this sudden revelation. "How often does it come?"

"Every two weeks."

"When was the last time?"

He paused to think, his brow straining as he counted back in his mind.

"Two days before I found you. So it'll be back again a week from now."

"Would you take me to it?"

"Sure."

"What city does it come from?"

"People just call it the city now but my mum said they used to call it LA."

The realisation that home was closer than she could ever have imagined made butterflies tear at Eva's stomach.

"And are you sure it's okay for me to stay here that long?" she asked, trying to keep a clear head.

"Yeah." said Matthew. After he did so, the excitement visibly drained from his face as he slowly sank back into the chair upon which he sat. Eva immediately knew the cause for his sudden sadness; he did not want to be alone again.

"Come with me." she said; her tone even more excited and decisive than before.

"What?"

"Come with me to the city. We can go together."

"But your family…"

"They'd be happy to have you. Besides, I want you to come."

"Really?" he asked. Exhilaration seeped its way back into his demeanour as a smile returned and he leant towards her, small hands gripping the arms of the chair.

"Yeah, of course. It's the least I owe you after everything."

"Thanks Eva." he said quietly. His eyes were dazed with anticipation. The prospect of continued companionship and a way out of the isolated woodlands was clearly one that brought great joy.

Eva too began to smile. For the first time since her betrayal at the hands of Thomas and Delilah, she finally felt she had a genuine chance to make it back home. After an hour or so of further talking, Matthew blew out the remaining candles and curled up under a blanket on the chair. Eva lay back and quickly slipped into a deep sleep; only that night, her dreams were not plagued by men from 'Station 12'; nor needles, fear and running but rather filled with images of reuniting with her mother and father; her new friend Matthew standing by her side.

Chapter Fourteen

The next morning, Eva woke from the best night's sleep she could ever recall with a smile still firmly in place. Matthew had evidently already left to do his morning's work, as the room was empty. He was good at coming and going undetected; silently tiptoeing around so as not to disturb Eva's rest. The comforting and now very much familiar beam of light was funnelling in through the open door.

    For around a week now, she had rested her leg as solidly as she could to try and aid the healing process, only getting up with the aid of Matthew when she had to use the bathroom – or rather a bucket – to relieve herself: Unappealing and embarrassing at one time perhaps but perfectly common practice these days. There was only one more week in which she could recuperate before she and Matthew would need to set out to meet the supply truck and make their way into what was once Los Angeles. She knew therefore that a few days of further rest would likely be the best option before she began to take her first tentative steps since the injury was sustained. Temptation however, proved too powerful. Having felt trapped indoors for far longer than any one person should be for the past eight months, she craved the rejuvenation of fresh air and open space.

The bandages rubbed against her leg, irritating her delicate skin. Though Matthew helped to redress the healing wound every couple of days, the itching on this morning was almost too much to tolerate. With the open doorway to the outside world an invitation that could no longer be ignored, she had to get up. Placing one hand on the edge of the bed and the other on the wall beside the pillow, she swung her legs round. Though she placed her right foot against the floor without pause, she hesitated somewhat in putting her left leg under pressure. With a wince, she gradually eased it onto the floor. She found the abrupt coldness of the hard ground against her bare feet somewhat welcoming and utterly refreshing in comparison to the now stale warmth of the bed to which she had been confined. With her boots lying discarded at the other side of the room, she opted not to try and reach them and would instead make straight for the door.

Still using the mattress and the wall for support, Eva hoisted herself up. The resulting stab of pain shot from her calf right up through her thigh and into her hip. With a jolt and a gasp, she lifted her left leg ever so slightly from the ground and balanced on her right. The relief from the pain was immediate. Having not even stood unaided, let alone walked, for so long, both legs felt strange and prickled with a slight numbness. After a few deep breaths, she began to hobble towards the door, putting as little weight as possible on her left leg.

Reaching the doorway, she grabbed onto either side of the frame. Her eyes were bombarded by blindingly white light that descended from the glorious sun. One by one, trees and bushes began to come into focus as her vision adjusted to the intense light she had been shielded from for so long. It allowed memories of her initial escape from 'Station 12' to flash into her mind for a brief moment but she quickly pushed them out again, deciding instead to focus on finding Matthew.

With the gentle rustle of the wind winding its way through the undergrowth and the chorus of birds overhead, she felt reassured that the surrounding area was safe enough to explore. Remembering that Matthew told her the vegetable garden was located behind the cabin, she pushed her way through the few remaining vines that dangled in front of the entrance and began to make her way around, placing her right hand against the concealed wall and using it as a guide to support herself. From a distance, the entire cabin would be completely invisible, fading into the background due to the skilful way it had been embedded into the land and coated in natural life.

At the back of the secret cabin was a dirt path leading into a cluster of trees. With nature's symphony still in full performance, Eva felt brave enough to venture in alone. With the wall no longer present to provide support, she slowed her pace, an occasional dull ache pulsing through her left leg as she moved.

Having followed the path, Eva emerged in another small clearing, bathed in sunlight from above, yet guarded from the elements by the surrounding shield of trees; the perfect spot for a vegetable garden. Sure enough, in the middle of the plot, Matthew knelt, tending to the crops that grew within. Just to the side of the garden was a trough, which Eva assumed was positioned to collect falling rain water.

Suddenly alerted to the fact that he was being watched, Matthew jolted to his feet and spun around, a look of panic upon his face. So innocent and fearful was this look that Eva could not help but feel a great wave of sadness for this young boy who had been forced to survive alone for all this time.

"Sorry." said Eva in a quiet voice, "I didn't mean to creep up on you."

"Oh… That's okay." said Matthew, "What are you doing out here? Your leg…"

"I needed to stretch it. You know, cabin fever." she replied, with a slight tilt of her head and a soft smile to reassure the startled youngster.

Matthew wiped the dirt from his hands onto his washed out, grey T-shirt and walked towards Eva.

"Do you need to sit down?" he asked; his eyes full of concern.

"Yeah, thanks."

With Matthew's help, Eva sat on the grass by the side of the garden, her legs outstretched in front of her. Placing her hands behind her for support, she leaned back, closing her eyes and allowing the sun to bathe her face in warmth. The wondrous sights, sounds and smells of Mother Nature seemed more abundant to Eva than ever before. She completely immersed herself in them once more while Matthew finished tending to the vegetables.

Under Eva's instruction, Matthew removed a few potatoes, a handful of carrots, an onion and a leek from the soft ground and took them round to the fire pit by the front of the cabin. Along with a small amount of water that had gathered in the trough, Eva boiled the finely chopped vegetables over an open fire to make the duo soup for their supper.

Matthew finished his in a mere few minutes; the soup evidently the first cooked meal he had eaten for quite some time. Once both had finished the contents of their bowls, Eva dished out the remaining helping to her young companion, which he accepted gratefully following some persuasion.

With full and satisfied stomachs, they relaxed and watched as the sun retreated behind the hilltops and the stars began to illuminate the night sky. Before they headed back inside, they chatted once again. This time however, the topic of discussion was not memories from their past lives but of their hopes and excitement for the future once they escaped the forest and reunited with Eva's parents.

The next morning, Eva resolved to use their remaining days to practice walking. With Matthew explaining that the journey would take almost a day, she knew she would either have to have healed her leg by easing through the pain or at least have become accustomed enough to the discomfort to be able to press on regardless; this was her one opportunity to get as far away as possible from 'Station 12' and get one step closer towards finding her mother and father and with the increasing amount of movement she could feel within her ever blossoming stomach, she knew there could not be too long left before her baby would be born; a thought that terrified her and which she tried very hard not to dwell on for long due to how fast it made her heart beat.

For the next four days that followed, Eva used a stick that Matthew had fetched for her as a cane to aid her rehabilitation. While he tended to the vegetables, scouted the area for intruders and gathered water from the trough, Eva walked around the cabin and explored its surrounding areas; always making sure to stay within shouting distance of Matthew should danger emerge. Luckily for them both, it never did.

By the fifth day, the time had come to set off to meet the supply truck. Though there had been a noticeable improvement in the condition of Eva's leg, she opted to continue using the stick for additional support. With an air of excitement surrounding the duo, they set off first thing in the morning while the sun was high and the day would offer as much light as possible to guide them on their way. Armed with a rucksack that contained a bottle of water and what vegetables were left from the garden, Matthew led the way without a single glance or word of farewell to what had for so long, been his home. Though at first this struck Eva as being somewhat strange, she soon identified with the loneliness the young boy had come to associate with the cabin. In many ways, it had been as much of a prison to him as 'Station 12' had been for her.

With the bustle of nature as their marching song, the friends walked on side by side; both seeking to leave behind the demons of their past in search of a better future just as much as the other.

Chapter Fifteen

The pair made their way through the woodland without much communication; not because of tension but merely so they could conserve their energy and press on as quickly as possible. Having now been together uninterrupted for around two weeks, Eva and Matthew felt entirely comfortable in each other's company.

Every couple of hours, they would find a suitable resting spot - usually in the shade of a large oak tree - and rehydrate with a few small sips of water. The air was warm and Eva's body prickled with tiny beads of sweat; carrying her own bodyweight on her injured leg would have been tricky enough but the additional strain of the baby growing within her made the journey even more strenuous. She refused to complain however, as she knew very well that reaching the supply truck on time was of paramount importance and with the excitement and anticipation written all over Matthew's face, she did not want to risk worrying him or tainting his long awaited return to civilisation; an event he would undoubtedly have dreamt of several times during his time in isolation.

A trickle of vibrant red stained the previous white of the bandages wrapped around her wound; blood was gradually seeping its way through. She breathed her way through the pain and tried to conceal it from her expression; having been walking for hours, she knew they had to be getting close by now.

You can rest on the truck. You can rest on the truck.

This was the single thought running through Eva's mind that sustained her relentless progress through the perilous forest. She flinched with every twig that grazed her skin and every rock that pressed into her feet but smiled in reassurance every time her young companion glanced back towards her to check if she was alright.

Soon the time came for another break. Spotting a nearby tree that had fallen to the ground, the pair headed for it and propped themselves against it for support. Eva could tell that Matthew was tired as well but it was not enough to dent his evident joy. He took the rucksack from his back and dropped it to the ground with a sigh of relief. Bending forwards, he began to massage his aching legs; Eva wished she could do the same but did not dare touch her tender calf, which was now pulsating yet feeling increasingly numb, making her whole leg tingle.

"You thirsty?" Matthew asked, his question breaking the silence.

"Yeah, very." she replied, laying her walking stick on the ground.

Unzipping the bag, Matthew pulled out the water bottle, now with only about half of its contents remaining. He handed it to Eva and she began to drink, allowing herself more than on previous rest stops. Her thirst feeling at least partially quenched, she handed the bottle back to Matthew. He glanced from the bottle to Eva and then swiftly put it back inside his bag.

Eva immediately knew that her friend was sacrificing a drink for himself so as to allow her to drink more later on their journey. Though grateful at his generous gesture, she could not accept such selflessness. Before she even had time to open her mouth to argue, the sound of a branch snapping rang out through the trees. In a sudden commotion, the undergrowth burst into life as birds squawked and fled the scene. A flurry of crisp, red leaves cascaded around the duo, having been savagely torn from their trees as their inhabitants hurried to safety.

Silence soon returned and neither Eva nor Matthew uttered a word but for a fleeting moment, their eyes met and both knew that they shared the exact same fear.

Sure enough, a group of four men emerged not twenty yards from where they stood. Dressed all in black and clutching guns, Eva recognised them at once. Without a sound, both Eva and Matthew clambered over the fallen tree which had been their resting post and crouched down behind it.

Eva's breathing was heavy and her hands clamped onto her stomach. Glancing over to Matthew ready to comfort him, she expected to find the youngster trembling with fear, yet it was he who seemed composed and poised for action. Peering over the log for a moment, he quickly ducked back into cover and turned to face Eva. Placing his hands on her shoulders and looking deep into her eyes, he spoke with a low voice full of clarity and not so much as a hint of doubt.

"They're heading this way. I have to distract them."

"What do you mean?" asked Eva, wishing her voice could sound as fearless as his.

"They'll find us. Your leg, you can't run. I can lead them away, then double back and meet up with you."

"No Matthew, you can't. We have to stay together."

"We don't have much time Eva. Make sure you

get back to your parents, okay? Just find the stream and follow it west. The truck will be at the end of it."

Without time for Eva to even think about the sudden change in their circumstances let alone answer him, Matthew stood up and leapt over the fallen tree that stood between them and their adversaries. Eva pitifully outstretched a hand towards where he had been not a moment before but it all happened too quickly for her to stand any chance of influencing his decision.

"Over there!" shouted one of the men. "That's the little shit who attacked me. He knows where she is." At once, a barrage of thunderous footsteps was all that could be heard as the soldiers set out in pursuit of the young hero. Waiting long enough to know that their attention was well and truly away from where she hid, Eva looked up over the top, her hands gripping tightly to the bark of the tree.

Matthew was tearing his way through the woodland, skilfully winding in and out of the trees to avoid the bullets now piercing their way through the air towards him. Every shot sent a jolt through Eva's heart as she flinched in fear for her friend.

One man stopped running and lifted his rifle up to eyelevel, steadying his aim. A shot rang out that seemed louder than all those that had come before it. All else seemed to disappear from the scene as Eva's eyes focussed in on Matthew's small, lifeless body falling to the ground.

Chapter Sixteen

Frozen with shock, Eva slid back under the cover of the fallen tree. She did not scream; she did not cry. Instead, she knelt, motionless. Her eyes blurred out of focus as she lost the consciousness to even blink. Her breathing was slow and shallow.

Though she would not dare to look even if her body granted her the ability to do so, she could hear the soldiers in the midst of a heated discussion. Only occasional words managed to penetrate their way into her numbed mind; the rest all morphing into a solid mass of chaotic noise. Though she did not garner enough information to determine their next move, she knew that Matthew's killer was being reprimanded for his actions. Perhaps their shots were intended to wound and capture; not yet to kill. Somehow those fleeting thoughts were not of any comfort.

It took several minutes of silence for Eva to process that her hunters had left the area. In a sudden jolt of awareness, she rose to her feet and clambered out of her hiding spot. With no regard for safety or even a quick scan of her surroundings, she ran towards Matthew, eyes fixed on his still and frail body.

Upon reaching him, she fell to her knees and the situation overwhelmed her as tears forced their way from her eyes. Matthew lay face down; his back punctured by the gunshot wound that had ended his life. His grey T-shirt was now splattered with ruby red, as blood continued to seep from his fatal injury.

"I'm so sorry." said Eva, placing a hand on top of his. Her voice was broken and shaking as she struggled to speak through the tears and the piercing pain in her heart that was far greater than any physical pain she had endured throughout her journey.

The indignity of his position was now what pained her the most. Looking around, she spotted a nearby branch that lay discarded on the ground. Picking it up, she began using the sharpened edge where it had once been attached to its tree as a spade to scrape at the soft ground underfoot. At this time, the supply truck was of no concern and reuniting with her parents could wait; all that mattered to Eva was burying her friend and having the chance to say goodbye.

Her heavy bump slowed her down and sweat seemed to ooze from every pore of her body but she pressed on. Owing to Matthew's age and undernourished body, the grave would not have to be very big; a small saving grace among the clouds of sadness that engulfed the situation.

As she continued to dig, Eva pictured the smile that had been spread across Matthew's face since they set off from the cabin just a matter of hours ago; how excited he had been to leave the forest behind and return to what remained of society, armed with a new companion; but what hit her most of all was how quickly he had so selflessly sacrificed it all to protect her.

Wiping the sweat from her brow with her forearm, she threw down the branch and pulled herself out of the hole she had spent the last hour or so digging. She panted heavily and her knees quivered from exhaustion but giving up was not an option. Bending forwards and placing her hands on Matthew's shoulders, she rolled him onto his back. Though his body was now cold and his skin seemed so pale it was almost translucent, his eyes were closed and a strange look of calm was upon his face; he looked peaceful and this at least was a welcome surprise to Eva.

Picking him up in her arms, she was astonished at

how light the boy was; his months of solitude and little food having evidently taken their toll. She could feel the bones of his ribcage digging into her hands as she delicately lowered him into the shallow hole. Though she knew the guilt and sadness at his death would continue to burden her soul for a long time to come, a part of Eva felt strangely relieved as she began to push the earth back in place. As terrible as she felt for thinking it, as Matthew's body gradually disappeared into the ground, Eva took comfort in knowing he would at least no longer suffer as a result of the world that was falling apart around them.

The finishing touch was to pluck a handful of small, white flowers from a cluster that blossomed nearby. Kneeling down one last time, Eva placed them on top of the freshly covered hole that now served as Matthew's final resting place.

With the knowledge that he had died so that Eva and her unborn child could go free, she got to her feet once more and though she had a heavy heart to add to her woes, she resolved not to allow the youngster's death to have been in vain. With a final glance towards her friend's makeshift grave, she turned and continued towards the drop-off point for the supply truck; her last and only hope of ever truly escaping the clutches of 'Station 12' and the destructive power of the government.

Chapter Seventeen

The true determination of Eva's former captors to halt her escape was now undeniable. The murder of a child purely due to his association with their target had taken the situation to a whole other level of fear. Rather than reduce her to a feeling of inevitable failure however, this served only to instil within Eva an equally growing determination of her own to reunite with her family and expose the secrets of 'Station 12'. Perhaps America had known about their endeavours to a greater extent than she could ever have anticipated but this evidently was not enough; the world had to know.

Desensitised to the pain of her injured leg, she pushed through the thriving forest, oblivious to the previously irritating nicks and scrapes of hostile branches. Unblinking, she pressed on as quickly as she could in the direction Matthew had explained the truck's destination would be located just moments before his death.

With every few steps came the image of the young boy's body, so vivid in her mind. Swallowing hard, she did all she could to force the thoughts out; now was not the time to grieve. Eva knew if she were to miss the truck, all of their effort – not to mention Matthew's sacrifice – would have been entirely wasted. More prevalent was the fear of being stranded alone in the depths of the woodland once again; with the soldiers of 'Station 12' in constant pursuit, her likelihood of survival was dwindling with every passing second she remained within their vicinity. With the impromptu burial throwing her journey off schedule and with no friends left to aid her efforts, everything rested upon reaching this truck on time and fleeing to the city. Whether her hunters intended to capture or kill her, she did not know for sure, but neither were outcomes she was willing to accept without every attempt to evade them she could muster.

The familiar scrape of a dry throat soon returned, bringing home the realisation that Eva had forgotten to collect Matthew's bag full of supplies before her departure. Once again finding herself without food or water, the pain that struck with each swallow reminded her of her previous attempts to run through the woods in search of freedom; only this time, her efforts were at least not without definite aim: Reach the stream and follow it west to find the dirt path; that is where the truck will be. With Matthew's final instructions replaying in her mind, it become clear that he had known Eva would likely have to undertake the rest of the journey alone; his sacrifice fully intended and not merely a tragic accident.

Just as the coldness of her inner grief began to engulf her mind, Eva shook her head and freed herself from its menacing grip. From then she resolved to maintain one thought and one thought only until she had seen out her mission: *Get to the truck.*

Just a few minutes more and she came to a sudden stop. Straining her neck to listen and holding her breath for a moment, her hope was confirmed. Through the sound of the whistling wind came the glorious trickle of running water. Breaking into as close to a sprint as her injured leg and exhausted body would allow, she ran towards the noise.

She emerged in yet another clearing surrounded by trees, complete with the welcome sight of a gentle stream; its crystal clear water flowing over smooth rocks of all shapes and sizes. Using the small patch of grassy land by the very edge of the stream, she headed west as per Matthew's advice. With the pain in her throat not even enough to tempt her into stopping to quench her thirst, the knowledge that her destination was within reach took complete and unyielding hold.

Get to the truck. Get to the truck.

Around each meander she strained in the hope of catching a glimpse of the truck or at least the dirt road which it would use to arrive. Though this final stretch of her journey seemed to Eva to last a lifetime, it was only a matter of minutes before the stream could be seen descending into a climactic pool at the end of its flow. At its finish was a dusty old pathway faintly marked by the wheels of a vehicle. Gathered around the pool were a cluster of people. Dressed in torn, faded clothes that resembled those that had belonged to Matthew, these people were evidently civilians awaiting the obviously imminent arrival of the supply truck. Matching Matthew's descriptions perfectly, a few of the group were brandishing baskets full of freshly grown vegetables to be traded for medical supplies from the city.

Eva counted at least ten members of the group and though no security personnel could be seen among them, a quick glance down to her stomach and a fleeting memory of how her encounter with Thomas and Delilah Cain had ended were enough to make up her mind. Ducking back into the cover of the trees, she crept close enough to get a full view of the scene before her. Crouching behind a thorn bush, she peered out at the faces of the group, each one as vacant and full of sorrow as the next. Like Eva, they waited in silence. With her hesitance to trust the people before her, she knew few were likely to share in the innocence and generosity of Matthew and with the risk of failing at the last hurdle absolutely not an option, she knew her best hope would be to wait for the trucks arrival and for the crowd to satisfy their trading needs before clearing the area. Then, she would find a way to board the truck and finally bid this woodland prison farewell. With her plan firmly in place, she poised herself, ready to move whenever the timing was right.

Chapter Eighteen

Enough time passed for Eva's breathing to return to its normal rate, no longer requiring her to resist the urge to gulp at the air around her. With this composure came the validation of her body's fatigued state. Having forced all else from her mind except her determination to reach her destination on time, she had somehow managed to block out the searing pain that now pulsed through her legs: Her left leg prickled around the area of her wound, the bandage soiled with a mixture of blood and dirt. Her right leg was also uncomfortable, the strain of supporting its injured counterpart finally beginning to take its toll. The burning sensation that engulfed her throat with each swallow made her face screw up in light of the effort this normally simple task now required. In spite of her ailments however, Eva's resolve was no less intact; her eyes fixed on the people waiting below.

In the time that elapsed during her wait, she began to study each member of the group. There were in fact eleven of them; seven male and four female. The men all had the same basic look: worn out jeans with occasional tears in the denim around the knees; bulky boots on their feet and plain, dull coloured T-shirts soiled by stains. Most had stubble, with shaving and general care for appearance far from anyone's priority these days.

The women amongst them were equally as drab. Most of them also wore denim jeans and faded old tops while one of them wore an oversized sweater that had clearly belonged to a man. Her arms were folded across her chest and on her left hand Eva made out what appeared to be a wedding ring. She wondered if the sweater belonged to the woman's husband. If so, was he one of the men among the group? Was he even still alive?

The youngest member of the group, a girl Eva estimated to be around sixteen years old, was wearing a summer dress decorated with floral print that floated delicately around her pale legs. Though most of the pattern's detail had long since worn away, it remained pretty and uncharacteristically feminine when compared to the clothes of the others around her. A brief smile flashed across Eva's face; the thought of a young girl doing what little she could to hold onto her identity came as a warming thought.

The girl's long, blond hair flowed freely in the gentle breeze that swept through the clearing. Having evidently been deprived of products and treatments for some time, it formed tight ringlets that danced around her shoulders. On her feet she wore a pair of brown hiking boots. They appeared to be too big for her and the frayed laces trailed on the ground behind her. Before The Breakdown such footwear would have seemed strange on a young girl but dainty shoes had no place in this world. In her arms she cradled a basket full of freshly grown vegetables. Specks of soil dispersed amongst the produce confirmed how recently they had been plucked from the ground.

To complete the now standard look for civilians, not a single member of the group smiled or attempted to engage the others in conversation of any kind. Matthew said these drop-offs happened on a regular basis, taking place every two weeks. This implied these people must have encountered each other numerous times in the past, yet none seemed pleased in any way to meet with the others once again. Did they not trust each other? Were all people now potential betrayers just as Thomas and Delilah Cain had been? Perhaps they just struggled to even feel happiness anymore; the realities of their new way of life just too difficult to deal with.

As these and many other questions began circulating around Eva's brain, a rattling noise interrupted the silence that had engulfed the scene. Just as the group all turned to look down the dirt path, Eva did the same. Her elevation gave her the optimum view, meaning she was the first to see the battered old truck making its way towards the group. The time had finally come.

Drawing to a close with its side facing the crowd, the truck's engine stuttered to a halt. The driver's door swung open and a man jumped down, immediately making his way towards the back of the vehicle. The man looked as though he was around thirty years old and his build was somewhat muscular and healthy compared to the others but in spite of this, his clothes were as worn and faded as those who had been so desperately awaiting his arrival.

A sudden burst of energy had rippled through the crowd; each one moved in close and formed a semi-circle around the driver, who now pushed up the metal shutter at the back of the small truck before clambering inside. Though she could not discern individual items being handed down to the people, they appeared to be small boxes filled with bandages and other basic medical supplies. Old, musty blankets were given to each of the three older women, while a couple of men received walking boots (though they seemed to be in better condition than the ones they currently wore, they too were clearly second hand). Eva was unsure how the driver was deciding which items to dispense to each person but the thought soon drifted from her mind.

Very few words seemed to be being exchanged, though the occasional, mumbled 'thank you' was audible over the hustle and bustle of the now excitable crowd. Once the driver had distributed all he had to offer, the crowd began handing him their payment; baskets and boxes filled with rustic looking fruits, vegetables and herbs as well as the occasional dead rabbit.

The entire trading time drew to a close within a few minutes and the crowd soon began to disperse; though some headed off in twos, most – including the young, blond girl, went alone, having most likely been sent on behalf of what remained of their family. Then a solemn thought occurred to Eva; perhaps each of them was living alone just as Matthew had been.

With no time to dwell on the consideration, Eva refocused her mind and slowly began to creep from behind the thorn bush which had concealed her from view. As the last of the group disappeared into the surrounding trees, the driver jumped down from the back of the truck and pulled the shutter down behind him. He began to make his way around to the side of the vehicle and as soon as he moved behind it, Eva slid her way down the steep banking and onto the dirt path. The sound of the driver's door slamming shut and the engine roaring to life sent Eva's heartbeat into a frenzy; in seconds, her chance of escape would be gone with no possible reprieve for a further two weeks.

Running to the shutter, she grabbed hold of the handle and pushed upwards as gently as she could. Creating a gap that was just enough for her to squeeze through, she pulled herself into the truck, grunting as she did so. The ferocity of the vehicle's battered engine provided enough cover noise for Eva to slide the shutter back in place undetected. A second later, the vehicle jostled as the driver turned the truck and began driving back towards the city.

Plunged into darkness, Eva felt her way around the newly piled up boxes of vegetables and made her way to the back of the storage space. Sitting with her back against the wall, she sighed and the tension in her muscles swiftly began to subside. Placing both of her hands on her stomach; she closed her eyes and tilted her head back, resting it against the side of the truck.

In a hushed voice she whispered, "We made it. We're finally going home."

Chapter Nineteen

The journey seemed to last for hours but was due in most part to Eva's own brewing anticipation. She had no plan of action for when she arrived; she had been so focussed on reaching the truck to get to the city that she had failed to consider her next move from there. All she knew was that every second on the road took her further from the clutches of 'Station 12'.

The faces of her parents were so vivid in her mind as the truck clattered its way along the remote pathway. Having been unconscious throughout the original journey to 'Station 12' all those months ago, she had no point of reference as to the distance or time involved from where they had set off but given that this journey was undertaken on a fortnightly basis, she hoped this meant it would not be too substantial. With a stroke of luck, her parents would still live near the truck's drop off in former Los Angeles and someone who knew them could point her in the right direction. Though she knew the chance of this was slim, it was not enough to dampen the excitement within her at the prospect.

Nine months had now passed since Eva's selection to participate in the government's desperate attempt to save American civilisation. Since that day, she had neither seen nor heard from any of her loved ones. As if The Breakdown itself was not enough to draw her family together, the death of her older brother in the following riots made them grow even closer. It was impossible to survive alone in this world for long and her mother's relatively poor health at the time Eva was seized began to play on her mind once more. What if she had died? Eva would never have the chance to say goodbye. Her father would have been left alone; his wife and children having been taken from him. What if all this time she had been longing to return to a family that was no longer even alive?

As Eva's excitement began to descend into panic, she once again attempted to shake herself free from negative thoughts; something she had been forced to become good at doing during her time in captivity.

If she had managed to survive her ordeal, she was sure her mother could have recovered. After all, she had her father for support and the motivation to get well again in case of their daughter's return. With this new, positive outlook, anxious butterflies fluttered in Eva's stomach once again; or perhaps it was the baby moving. She could not tell for sure but whatever the cause, the realisation that the truck would soon have to reach its destination overwhelmed any lingering concern in her mind.

The driver would likely be shocked when he pulled open the shutter and found her there but Eva hoped his surprise would buy her enough time to jump down and flee the scene before too much attention was drawn.

Stretching her hands out in front of her, she gripped onto the top of a cold, wooden box and pulled herself up. Once standing, she tentatively felt her way back towards the shutter. Finding it, she waited, knees bent ever so slightly, poised for her quick getaway.

Around five minutes of waiting in this position and the truck came to an abrupt halt. The vehicle lurched, causing Eva to lose her balance. Thrusting her arms out, they hit against the shutter with a clatter and she managed to steady herself. The sound of the driver slamming his door shut soon came. Murmurs could be heard from the other side along with a quick succession of footsteps as the driver approached the back of the truck.

Light flooded in as the barrier between Eva and

the world was pulled up. Blinking away the blindness, the crowd of gathered people – at least three times the size of the one in the woodland – quickly came into view.

Eva did not jump down and run as she had expected she would, nor were the startled stares of the audience enough to spur her into any kind of action. She was vaguely aware that the driver was shouting something at her but his words failed to make their way in. For all the commotion of the scene before her, Eva was transfixed on one thing and one thing only. With the same big, blue eyes and long, dark hair; there, in the middle of the crowd staring directly at her, was the face of her mother.

Chapter Twenty

What happened next was all something of a blur to Eva. The arms of the driver gripped her wrists tightly and pulled her down from inside the truck. People were shouting and fussing over her; groping at her hair and touching her stomach. The sounds around her were muffled, failing to make any impact. The momentum of the crowd swarming in towards her pushed her forwards. For a moment her mother's face disappeared behind that of a much older woman who had been visibly haggard by a long and difficult life.

The sudden absence of her mother from her line of vision was what finally shocked Eva back to a feeling of awareness to the commotion of the scene. Her senses were engulfed by the situation she now found herself fully immersed in. Cold dry hands were clutching at her skin; shouts and gasps of disbelief surrounded her. Enclosed within the swelling mass of bodies, the smell of sweat was rife.

The face of the elderly woman was still before her and though the sudden bombardment of people had sent Eva's heart into a flurry of fear, it was immediately pacified by the warm expression spread across the woman's dilapidated features. She was smiling.

In an instant, Eva's mind seemed to separate the roar of the crowd into individual and discernible voices. Rather than the hostile shouts of hatred and anger she believed she had heard at first, she was instead greeted with cheers and words of celebration. The hands, once dangerous and imposing, suddenly felt kind and welcoming. They were pleased to see her. More than pleased, they were elated. All at once Eva knew these people understood exactly where she had just travelled from and what she would likely have gone through to be able to be standing here with them now.

Her eyes began to dart around the crowd, meeting the stares of her sudden admirers. Some were applauding; others had faces stained with tears. A number of the individuals registered within her memory and she knew they were people whom she had known at least vaguely before her imprisonment, though in the moment she could not place them to a name; each memory blurring with the next in one mass of confusion.

When her eyes returned to the elderly woman, her grin now broader than before, a hand reached out from behind her, trying desperately to force its way through the crowd. When a small gap briefly appeared, the panicked face of her mother soon returned to her sights, confirming her to be the owner of the outstretched hand.

"Mum!" screamed Eva, her strained voice cracking into a soft squeak; her own hand reaching out in return.

All but a few inquiring whispers, the sounds of the crowd faded and the bustle came to an immediate halt. Following Eva's gaze and outstretched arm, the crowd in unison turned to see Eva's mother. Once again acting as a whole, they took several steps back, at last creating a clear path between mother and daughter.

With several hurried paces towards each other, Eva fell into her mother's arms, her knees crashing against the dusty ground. Her mother was also on her knees, her arms cradled around her child, rocking her gently. Both were sobbing, their shoulders heaving from the power of their emotional outpouring.

The swarm did not seem to know how best to react to this unexpected turn of events and if they spoke at all, neither Eva nor her mother heard it. All that mattered to each of them in that moment was the person they held in their arms. The warmth of her mother's body against hers; the warmth she had so desperately craved for nine, long months; was more encompassing and wholly embracing than Eva had imagined in all the time they had been kept apart.

They remained this way for several minutes, not speaking; just being. Only becoming aware of the still present audience when a hand gently touched each of them on the shoulder, Eva looked up to find they belonged to the driver of the truck that had facilitated her escape. He too wore a smile full of sincerity and kindness.

"Come on." he said, "You can't stay here. I'll take you home."

As though struck by a sudden sense of urgency, Eva's mother stood up, the joy draining from her face. Taking hold of one arm each, she and the driver helped Eva to her feet. She did not need to enquire as to the need for haste. At any moment, a member of the government's security could arrive upon the scene, bringing Eva's new found freedom to an abrupt halt and a tragic end to the spontaneous celebration.

With one last glance around the area, Eva noticed that not all of the party had been so welcoming after all. Beyond the group of well-wishers still adorned with smiles and hands clasped as though in prayer, she could see a second, smaller group of people separating themselves from the others. As they slowly departed from the scene, their glances back met directly with Eva's; their eyes full of the same wildness that had consumed Thomas Cain right before he had gripped his gun and given chase.

Freeing her from the growing anxiety of another betrayal, her mother's voice spoke out to her for the first time since the morning of Eva's fateful meeting with the government officials. Full of all the same love and warmth as she had remembered, she could not help but smile as she heard it.

"Come on. Let's go home."

Chapter Twenty-One

Few words were exchanged throughout the journey. Mother and daughter merely gripped hold of each other's hands and huddled together as tightly as they could. The driver had led them back to the truck; though this time they sat on the large seat next to his, rather than crouching in the dark as Eva had done during her earlier trip from the woodland. He required little direction from Eva's mother as to where her home was located, just an occasional reminder of which turnoff to take. Their casual tone during these sporadic exchanges and her mother's immediate willingness to accept his offer of a ride confirmed to Eva that they must know each other fairly well. Were they merely familiar with each other from the fortnightly delivery of supplies or were they friends? Now did not seem the appropriate time to ask.

The question did not linger in her mind for long either. With her head resting on her mother's shoulder, she breathed in the familiar scent of the soap her family had always used to bathe themselves. Such luxuries were hard to come by these days but her mother, Alexandra Cole, had worked as a chemist before The Breakdown, specialising in herbal remedies. Her extensive knowledge of the plant life now abundant in the overgrown world could be put to good use when it came to concocting her own natural soaps, shampoos and rustic skincare products. Occasionally she would sell them along with freshly brewed herbal teas to other civilians in exchange for crops to make food with or materials to produce clothes, since money was of no use anymore. Regardless, it meant that Eva's family and their small home had been spared from smelling of stale sweat and earth, as the rest of the world and its inhabitants now seemed to. Thus, the smell had always reminded her of her family and having been kept from it for so long, it seemed that much sweeter, offering more reassurance now than it had ever done before.

The truck continued to make its way along the winding roads, leaving the city behind. Crumbling buildings were soon replaced with trees, shrubbery and open fields. The sun was beginning to set over on the horizon, an orange glow seeping its way across the land.

Questions began to enter Eva's mind; questions she so desperately longed to ask her mother but the words failed to come, her mind still heavy from the emotional overhaul of the last twenty-four hours. She decided to stop trying, figuring they were perhaps best kept for when they were home anyway. Home; a place that for so long had felt like it existed only in her mind; a place she scarcely allowed herself to think of through the fear of never being able to return; the place that came into view as the truck headed up a dirt road and entered into a small clearing.

Eva's eyes began to sting with tears at the sight before her. Aside from a little more general wear and the mossy coating that tarnished many a building since The Breakdown, the small structure built from thick wood by her father's own hands, was just as she had remembered it. Surrounded by trees, her father had chosen to move them here shortly after The Breakdown first began, surmising that it was secluded enough from the heart of the city to keep them out of harm's way but close enough to civilisation that they could return for vital supplies whenever necessary. Eva had never expected her home to have been so close to 'Station 12' all this time. The revelation was equally as frustrating as it was a relief.

Aside from the small cluster of growing vegetables, the basic garden to the left of the house was abundant with the usual plants and herbs used in her mother's creations, while the right hand side played host to the small chicken coop surrounded by wire to keep them from escaping. Again, this had been created by Eva's father shortly after they moved here. Having spotted a number of wild chickens roaming the surrounding forest, he felt their best hope was to domesticate them and harvest their eggs, rather than try and hunt them individually. Initially he had planned to kill them off gradually to also provide meat but Eva's attachment to them soon led to the dismissal of the idea. All seven had been allowed to live unscathed, though Eva could only count five now as she climbed down from the truck, once again aided by the friendly hand of the driver.

"Thanks Declan." said Eva's mother, her voice sounding tired and strained. "Would you like to come in for some tea?"

"Thanks but that's okay. I imagine you have some pretty serious catching up to do."

"I owe something in exchange for your kindness at least. After all, I don't think we could have walked back all this way after… everything."

"It's fine. Really." said Declan, his handsome face once again playing host to a warm smile. "I'd better get back before it gets dark."

"If you're sure." Alexandra answered with a smile of her own.

Declan's attention switched from Alexandra to Eva but his smile remained unchanged as he looked into her eyes.

"Welcome home."

"Thank you." said Eva, "…for everything."

With one last glance to each of the women, Declan turned and headed back towards his truck. It roared to life and within a matter of seconds, had disappeared beyond the trees.

"Welcome home." said Alexandra, mirroring Declan's words as tears formed in the corners of her eyes.

"I never thought I would be here again." replied Eva. Her voice diminished to that of a child, shaking with the overwhelming swell of emotion pounding through her entire body.

"I can't believe you're here." Alexandra took her daughter's hand in hers as she spoke. "I love you so much. I can't imagine how your father will react when you walk back in that door unannounced after all this time."

Eva was struck at once by feelings of relief and guilt in equal measure: Relief at the knowledge her father was alive and well but guilty for having not asked for this information earlier. It was one of the many questions that had been hurtling through her mind at top speed during the journey home, when her mouth had failed to form the words she had so desperately sought to release.

The hens clucked obliviously as the two began to make their way towards the door at the front of the house. Alexandra opened it with one hand, the other still holding onto Eva. They entered into the living area of the small structure that served as both the kitchen and lounge. The furniture was arranged exactly how it had been before Eva's absence. The same table they gathered around each meal time. The same old cooker with a rusted hob that cooked their meals. The same musty, brown sofa against the back wall next to the side table that was adorned with a small, wireless radio. To anyone else this would seem a bare and barren cave that served the mere purpose of providing shelter against the elements but to Eva, this was home; the place she had longed to return to for nine long months.

The joy that rose within her was soon diluted by the nerves that crept their way in. Her face drained of colour and her palms became sticky with sweat.

"Alistair." Alexandra called out to her husband, her voice audibly affected by the same nerves brewing in Eva.

Just a few seconds later, Alistair appeared at the open doorway by the sofa that led to the small bedroom shared by him and Eva's mother. He too was silent, frozen to the spot upon which he stood. Draining of colour just as Eva had done mere moments before; his eyes were fixed upon his daughters'.

"Eva?" Alistair's deep, powerful voice had always made Eva feel safe; its strong tone and liquid clarity a constant source of reassurance. With this question however, Eva heard it quiver with emotion for the first time since her brother's death three years ago.

"Dad..."

The sound of her voice threw him into motion, his mind regaining control over his body. Opening his arms he ran to his family, pulling both wife and daughter into his chest. They held each other tightly and clasped their eyes shut. All three were crying. The moment they had all independently dreamed of and longed for had been realised at last. The emptiness reflected in each of their souls for nine months filled once more. Finally, Eva was home.

Chapter Twenty-Two

The Cole family remained huddled as one until long after the sun had retreated behind the mountaintops once more. Alexandra was fussing over the stove, preparing a pot of one of her homemade herbal tea recipes to calm their nerves. Eva lay across the sofa, her head resting on her father's lap; her hands cradling her stomach, his running softly through her hair.

Each of them had been burdened by questions and worries for months, yet the immediacy of their reunion had resulted in something of a state of shock from which they could not break free. The whistle of the pot as it boiled was all that tainted the silence. The smell of mint drifted through the air and revived Eva from her drowsy demeanour.

She propped herself into a sitting position and accepted the mug filled with the freshly brewed tea from her mother. With just a single sip, her mouth was overcome with the vibrancy of flavours that danced across her tongue. The fresh, earthiness of the mint was accompanied by beautiful, sweet undertones of berries; she had forgotten just how delicious it was.

By now her father had risen from the sofa, offering to serve his own tea so that Alexandra could sit beside Eva. After all three of them had taken a few more sips each, their tears had dried and the tension had somewhat dissipated from the cool air. Placing his mug on the wooden table, tarnished with stains and scratches, Alistair crouched down in front of Eva and placed his hands on her knees. The look on his face was not imposing, nor unnerving, yet without a word managed to portray exactly what they all were thinking: They could not avoid discussing what had happened during Eva's absence any longer.

With the clarity of the meaning behind her father's stare, Eva was struck once again by a burning question; this one so pressing that it forced all others that had been swirling around in her mind for hours to the very back of her thoughts. Her heart rate began to rise until it was beating in her ears like a symphony of drums. Without time to consider a possible answer, she blurted out her question, eyes still fixed on her father's.

"Why haven't you asked me about the baby?"

The intensity of the emotions and overwhelming nature of their impromptu reunion had allowed even Eva to forget momentarily about the child growing within her but with this question came the realisation that neither of her parents, nor Declan, nor the gathering crowd of familiar faces that had surrounded her in town had asked her a single question or shown even an flash of surprise at her bulging stomach.

Alistair's eyes did not flinch but the expression across his face softened into a smile that calmed Eva's rising feeling of fright. Her mother's hand soon held hers and the worry and fear were replaced with an all-consuming sense of understanding: Just as Thomas and Delilah Cain had done, Eva's parents had known exactly what happened to her in 'Station 12'.

"Once you and the other girls summoned to the hearing didn't come home, people began to panic. Word spread and questions were asked." Alexandra's voice was steady as she re-told the facts as plainly as she could. "Once it was clear something was wrong, the threat of more riots was enough to make the government send out letters to the families."

As if to illustrate the truth behind his wife's words, Alistair rose and opened the drawer by the side of the stove, pulling out a piece of paper. Holding it out to Eva, she slipped her hand from her mother's hold to accept it, the other gripping tightly to the mug of warm tea. It was addressed to her parents and the governmental seal adorning the top left corner were enough to convince her of its authenticity. Her focus quickly returned to Alexandra as she resumed her story.

"They told us that our daughters had been selected as part of a vital fertility programme and that we should be proud to know they had been chosen." she scoffed as she spoke. "The letters said that the girls should be able to return within a year. Rumours spread pretty quickly and it didn't take long for people to work out what was going on."

"So everyone knew this whole time?" Eva asked; her voice laden with sorrow.

"Few people would talk about it outright but it was clear most people knew." It was Alistair who answered this time.

"I don't understand. If everyone knew, why were they so desperate to stop me escaping? They shot me in the leg." She glanced down at her bandaged wound as she spoke. "And they…" she trailed off, deciding it was still too soon for her to relive the memories of Matthew's death; that wound far rawer than any of the ones on her body.

"I wish we knew for sure." said Alexandra.

"They're most likely afraid that you'll tell the rest of the world." Alistair spoke again, taking the letter from Eva, carefully folding it up and placing it back in its drawer. "They don't even let people in and out of the country anymore, so I can't imagine they want everyone else knowing the sick measures they're taking to save their dying excuse for a country."

Though his words were full of the personal contempt he held for the government for what they had done to his daughter, they also made sense to Eva. Why else would they resort to trailing her through the forest for days and killing an innocent child on sight purely because he had been spotted with her? All at once, everything seemed to fit into place. With America's long held mistrust of the outside world and fear of involvement from foreign governments since The Breakdown, they truly were determined to contain the secrets of what happened behind the closed doors of 'Station 12' and the others like it.

"What if they come after me?" she asked.

"You're safe now Eva." said Alistair.

"Other people were summoned too, probably guinea pigs for other twisted experiments but the more people asked questions, the more hostile the government became." Alexandra's story was evidently not yet done, her hand clutching onto Eva again as they sat, side by side. "Your father even earned himself a beating for getting too heavy handed with one of the guards in town."

Again as if to illustrate her words, Alistair turned and lifted his shirt, revealing the pale scars covering his back. The sight made Eva wince. Though public whippings were rare, they were not unheard of when people showed signs of rebellion or distaste towards the government.

Lowering his grubby T-shirt to conceal his wounds, Alistair crouched down in front of Eva again, though this time his eyes were focussed on her stomach.

"Did they…"

His question remained unfinished but Eva knew all too well what he wanted to know.

"No." she answered.

The truth was Eva had been unconscious during her impregnation and had simply woken to be told she was with child and would from that point be closely monitored. Every few weeks she received a scan and her blood pressure was reviewed. Weekly 'treatments' had consisted of the red liquid injection that made her feel drowsy and lethargic; the same one she plunged into Johnson to initiate her escape. Having never been told the true nature of the process, she had forced herself to assume that even the corrupt and desperate government would never resort to actual, physical rape.

"You must be due any day now." said her father, a statement of fact rather than a question.

"Almost nine months now." she answered, grateful at least for the distraction from that thought, though she soon lowered her gaze to the floor and spoke the words she had so willed herself to contain ever since her apprehension.

"I'm scared."

For so long her priority had been escaping; freeing herself and her unborn child from the prying hands of 'Station 12's medical team. Only now did the prospect of raising a child in this desolate world finally begin to feel like a reality.

"You're not alone. We're with you every step of the way from now on. This baby is yours now and that's all that matters." Alexandra tightened her grip on Eva's hand as she spoke.

Memories and questions were so abundant they threatened to overflow her mind.

"But what if they do come after me?" she asked again. "The men from 'Station 12'."

"They won't." said her father, his voice unshaking.

"How can you be so sure?"

"You said yourself that they were desperate to stop you getting away. Why would they bother if they knew where to find you? I'm willing to bet those guys haven't got a clue who you or any of the others in there were or what the government's grand plan is. The reason they tried so frantically to stop you was so they didn't have to tell their bosses that they messed up. Now that you're gone, they'll want to keep as low a profile about all this mess as you do."

His words provided immediate relief and with a final few sips of tea, Eva decided that rest was her best option; her brain in need of a break from all the confusion.

Her parents led her into the small bedroom she had shared with her brother before his death. Though his bed had been removed to allow room to manoeuvre the space, Eva had retained his few other belongings as a reminder of his presence, including a framed photograph of the family that sat on the single shelf above her bed.

Everything was exactly how she had left it. The fresh smelling bed linen and distinct lack of dust evidence that her mother had kept the room clean in the hope of her daughter's eventual return. This thought made her smile ever so slightly.

With a kiss on the forehead and a lingering hug from each of her parents, they bid her goodnight and left the room to allow her to sleep. She immediately peeled off the jeans and white shirt, both tarnished by stains of blood and dirt. Wearing just her underwear and her bandages, she did not bother to find any clean clothes to replace them. Instead, she slipped under the duvet, the cool sheets soothing against her bare skin.

Her eyes soon felt heavy and began to flutter to a close. The length of the day, with its many surprises, had finally caught up with her. She just hoped the government never would.

Back in the kitchen, Alistair paced the room, his brow furrowed.

"Do you really believe what you just said back there?" asked Alexandra, her face equally as tainted by fear as that of her husband.

"We have to. There's no way Eva can cope with another trek through the woods; not in her condition. But put it this way, as soon as the baby is born and they're both strong enough, we're getting as far away from here as possible."

Chapter Twenty-Three

It was the sound of birds chirping and hens clucking that finally roused Eva from a dreamless sleep. She had not woken once from her slumber throughout the entire night, an extremely rare occurrence these days. The single window above the bed allowed light to bathe the small room in a warm, yellow glow. The sun was already high in the sky, the day fully underway.

Sitting up, she surveyed the yard in front of the house. The position and intensity of the light outside suggested it was around 11am; she had slept for a long time; the comfort of her old, familiar bed too much for her mind and body to resist yielding to. Her parents must have allowed her to sleep in, well aware of the much needed rest she would be catching up on. Glancing over to the door however, revealed it to have been left slightly ajar. Immediately she knew this would have been her mother's doing, so as to allow her to check on her daughter without the risk of disturbing her sleep.

A smile formed on Eva's face, the reality of being home for good beginning to sink in. A good night's rest allowed her to finally start to embrace and enjoy the bubbling feelings of happiness and freedom, rather than continue to live in perpetual fear that they were to be immediately snatched from her once more.

Swinging her legs from the bed, her feet found the floor and she stood, stretching her arms high above her head to set the tension in her muscles free. Her injured leg gave a familiar twinge as if to confirm that it had not yet fully healed but was marginally less painful than before. It was only now that she noticed the pyjamas that sat, neatly folded at the end of the bed, obviously left there by her mother in anticipation of her first night home. She quickly pulled on the cotton trousers and matching top, wanting her mother to feel her efforts had been fully acknowledged and appreciated.

She reached for the small chest of drawers, another handmade gift from her father on her sixteenth birthday. Opening the second from the top, she was greeted with the sight of her own clothes. The filthy, sodden offering from Delilah Cain still lay on the floor; Eva made a mental note to dispose of them before pulling out a white dress decorated with subtle orange flowers. It was one of her favourites and you would never have known it had been made by her mother almost two years ago from a large strip of material she had bought in exchange for three bars of soap and a handful of homemade herbal pain relief tablets. The finish was so clean and professional that any reputable tailor could have produced the dress before The Breakdown. The loose, flowing design of the garment would likely still allow it to fit over Eva's recently boosted frame. She removed a hand towel from the drawer below and clean underwear from the one at the top before heading into the kitchen.

Her mother was standing over the stove, the smell of porridge oats filling the room. Turning to see Eva in the doorway, she smiled.

"I can't tell you how nice it is to see you walking out that door again." she said.

"I can't tell you how good it feels to smell proper home cooking again." Eva responded; her face illuminated by a grin equally as enthusiastic as her mother's.

"I heard you getting up so I thought I'd fix you something to eat. You must be hungry by now."

"Starving." said Eva, placing her clean clothes on the sofa and taking a seat at the table. She would have to wait before she bathed and cleaned herself, the smell of the sweetened oats too delicious to ignore. Mixed with a splash of goats milk that was likely obtained by her father in exchange for a freshly killed rabbit from the woods, the bowl placed before her exuded streams of warmth. Within seconds, she had all but licked it clean.

With a gentle laugh, her mother offered her a second helping but Eva had not forgotten how scarce food could be and the absence of her father implied he was spending the day hunting, meaning he would be hungry upon his return. Resisting every inch of temptation that coursed through her veins, she rejected the offer for seconds with a polite smile and scooped up the pile of clothes from the sofa before heading out into the garden.

There was a trough behind the house, similar to the one that had been constructed outside Matthew's small makeshift home. On cold days, they would gather some water and heat it over the stove and take it to the bathroom to bathe there but on days like this when the sun beamed down in all its glory, they all agreed it was best to save the effort and simply bathe outside. With no windows on the back wall of the house and the rest of the area concealed by trees, it provided the perfect spot.

Still, Eva was eager to return to her mother's company and so made haste to remove her clothes and bathe her body using one of the spare scraps of material by the trough that now served its purpose as a flannel. The heat of the sun had warmed the water enough to take the edge from it, though it remained cool enough to feel refreshing; invigorating her skin and eliminating any lingering lethargy from her muscles following her long sleep.

She sparkled as the sunlight danced off the droplets of water coating her skin. Ever so gently, she peeled the bandages from around her leg, exposing the healing wound to the elements. The rush of cold air against the torn up flesh felt liberating but nothing compared to the divine pleasure of scooping her hand into the water and pouring it slowly down her calf.

The final step before patting herself dry was to grip tightly against the edge of the trough and plunge her hair into the water. The dark tresses spread out, carried by the gentle ripples. She wrapped the towel around her head and quickly pulled on her underwear before slipping the white dress on. To her relief, it still fit.

With a satisfied smile of familiarity at so suddenly resuming her old morning routine, she headed back towards the front of the house, surveying the signs of life among the surrounding trees as she went. Just as she was about to head inside, a rustle, louder than any she had heard while she had been bathing, rang out from somewhere nearby. Stopping, she whipped her head to the right, staring at the suspected source of the noise.

A second rustle came, this one louder than the last. Its cause was definitely too large to be a harmless mouse fleeing the scene or an injured bird fluttering through the bushes. No, this was something bigger and the emergence of a third rustling sound even louder than those before it confirmed it was moving ever closer to Eva.

Her lips poised to call for her mother as she began to take a step backwards. Images flooded her mind. Security men, dressed all in black, bursting from the trees brandishing weapons. Her mother screaming after her as she was dragged away to be returned to 'Station 12', or executed, or worse.

Just as the situation began to overwhelm her and her head felt dizzy with fear, a cat leaped from the treeline into the open. White, scruffy and with a split down the middle of its left ear, she recognised it immediately. Eva could not help but laugh as the sorry looking animal meowed up at her and brushed against her legs with its scraggily, white fur.

Scooping him up in her arms, she tickled him under the chin.

"Hello you." she said.

The response came in the form of a long, rough purr that sounded as though the cat had swallowed a mouthful of gravel. If encountering him for the first time, she would worry there was something wrong with him but the many hours they had spent in each other's company in the past had long since confirmed this was how he always sounded.

Their first encounter had indeed happened over three years ago during a hunting trip with her father. They had ventured deeper into the woods than usual that day, with game starting to become scarce in their usual search perimeter. They had heard a rustle similar to the ones just a moment ago, and just as her father had poised himself to plunge a spear into the animal lurking in the bushes, Eva had caught sight of a flash of white around a small face of frail whiskers.

Blood seeped from the open slash on its ear, with Alistair soon determining that the wound was too clean to have been inflicted by another animal. Alone, injured and frozen with fear, this kitten had evidently been attacked by a human.

Eva had sat with him, gently stroking his fear into submission as her father scoured the area in search of the animal's mother. With no luck, he considered killing it, not out of malice but simply to save it from a life of suffering and solitude. One look from Eva's wide, blue eyes filling with tears was enough to rule out that option and though her father was a generous man, he remained reluctant to take on the animal full time, wary of having an extra mouth to feed. He did however agree to spare the kitten's life and permitted Eva to take him home, clean his wounds and nurse him back to good health before setting him free once more.

After about a week, the kitten no longer winced when Eva's hand approached to comfort him and a few good meals had been enough to hide his ribcage from view under his fur, which was also no longer stained with blood. The split in his ear never closed up, though the potency of the wound seemed to fade with time. Against her father's best wishes, Eva nicknamed the animal Snowflake - Snowy for short - in homage to his beautifully uninterrupted white coat.

When the time came to return him to the woods from which he had come, Eva obliged with a heavy heart. Though Snowy too came to understand the arrangement, he would regularly return to the area and keep Eva company as she picked vegetables, gathered eggs from the hens or washed clothes in the trough. Every now and then, as though it were a special treat for them both, Eva would leave her bedroom window open just enough to allow Snowy to slip in once the sun had gone down. He would curl up beside her and, gravelly as it was, his purring would soothe Eva into a deep sleep.

Eva's father would often spot Snowy lounging by the trough on days when the sun was particularly hot or watching the chickens from the tree line as they pecked at their daily supply of grain. She came to suspect that her father soon caught on to Snowy's night time visits inside the house but thankfully it was never discussed. The animal's brutal introduction to the world and inbuilt natural instincts pushed him to learn to hunt for birds and mice, almost never accepting food from Eva even when she dared to try and sneak him some. Since he therefore proved himself to be of no burden to the family, his visits were allowed to continue without question.

Though both Eva and her new, furry friend evidently took comfort from the friendship, every once in a while, Snowy would disappear into the depths of the forest for several weeks; as though to remind himself never to become too reliant on his human companion. These absences worried Eva at first but she soon came to expect and understand them and it was during these weeks that Eva often wondered what betrayal had caused his initial abandonment in the woods all those years ago.

Three years on from that first encounter in the forest, Eva cradled Snowy in her arms, smiling down at him as he nuzzled against her.

"Sometimes I would find him sleeping in your room."

Eva turned to face the house and found her mother standing in the doorway.

"Really?" she asked.

"I guess your father and I weren't the only ones hoping you'd come home."

Eva carried the content cat into the kitchen. Having only ever been permitted entry into her bedroom since he was a kitten, his wide eyes took in the new sights while his nose twitched in response to the barrage of unfamiliar smells.

A pot simmered on the hob, a vegetable stew bubbling away for the evening's supper. It was rare to have two cooked meals in one day and without asking, Eva knew this was all in aid of her and though she considered it, protesting would be futile.

Hours passed with Eva finally finding the clarity to discern and ask the questions that had intermittently burdened her mind for so long, deciding now was as good a time as any to finally let loose her concerns and find closure to so many unresolved issues. She asked about her mother's return to good health, the growing resentment towards the government following her detainment and most of all about the people they considered friends from the town; the familiar faces that applauded her as she emerged, dazzled from the back of the supply truck the day before.

Just as the sun began to grow tired, Alistair entered through the open door, a makeshift spear in one hand; two dead rabbits in the other.

"Oh good." said Alexandra, taking the rabbits from his hand and laying them on the counter. "We're certainly dining well this week."

Alistair did not acknowledge his wife's words; instead he was staring at the ball of white fur curled up in Eva's lap.

"Is that thing still alive?" he asked.

Eva looked up at her father but the soft wink and subtle smile confirmed him to be joking, with Snowy welcome to stay. Though this surprised her at first, she soon wondered that if her mother had been aware of Snowy's presence during her captivity, perhaps her father had been too.

What Eva did not know was that two weeks after the government apprehended her, while her mother was still bedridden with illness; Alistair had entered her bedroom following a particularly lonesome day to find Snowy pacing Eva's bed. At first the two had frozen, staring at each other, unsure of how to respond but mere moments later Alistair held the animal in his arms, his tears mingling with the white fur of the cat whose life his daughter had convinced him to spare that day deep in the woods. Alistair soon fell asleep in Eva's room, exhausted from the trauma of the previous fortnight yet comforted that night at least by the company of Snowy, just as his daughter had been on many nights before him. Ever since then, he had grown decidedly more tolerant of

Snowy's presence, even tossing him scraps and bones every now and then from skinned animals when he spotted his big, green eyes watching him from just inside the treeline.

Oblivious to this information, Eva sat, convinced that her father was merely feeling generous since she had only just returned.

Following supper of Alexandra's delicious homemade stew, Snowy sat with the family on the sofa as they gathered to listen to the small radio in the corner of the room. The usual government propaganda and empty promises of a better future was all that filled the airwaves but most people still listened when they could, in the faint hopes of hearing something new. Of course there was never any mention of what was happening inside 'Station 12' or any of the others housing unwilling test subjects for their desperate measures to salvage what remained of their once glorious nation.

A full day having passed without any sign of her pursuers, Eva began to breathe more easily, the previously constant tension in her chest slowly relenting; the taste of freedom all the more sweet with each passing hour. With a yearning to experience the woods as she had done before her capture and wash away the new associations of danger and fear, she asked to accompany her father the following day on his usual hunting trip. He agreed with a gentle chuckle.

Bidding her parents goodnight for the second evening in a row, she made her way into her bedroom, an already sound asleep Snowy bundled in her arms. Laying him gently on his usual spot, she made sure this time to dress in the pyjamas neatly laid out for her by her mother before clambering under the thick duvet.

This night was not host to a dreamless sleep but one filled with friends and family; laughter and happiness. A smile spread across her face as Snowy curled up against her stomach, while the baby within her was kicking and wriggling, almost ready to be born.

Chapter Twenty-Four

The smile remained firmly on Eva's face as she woke from her slumber the next morning. Snowy was already awake, perched on the end of the bed and cleaning his face with his paws. His gravelly purr mingled with the songs of the birds that swept in through the open window. Eva ruffled the fur behind his ears and leant forward to give him a kiss. As if he had merely been waiting for his companion to awaken, he immediately let out a strained meow before clambering out the window and disappearing into the trees.

Eva dressed in the same white, floral dress she had worn the day before as clothing was limited and the luxury of a freshly laundered outfit every day had long since been forgotten. Just as she finished scraping her hair back into a ponytail and had secured it with a scrunchy made from interwoven scraps of old string, a sharp pain pulsed through her stomach. Clutching her sides, she grimaced and sat back on the edge of the bed.

Fear swirled around her and the room began to spin out of all recognition at the thought of going into labour. Her palms were slippery with sweat and her pulse pounded against her eardrums as she slowly massaged her stomach, swallowing as much air as she could. A few minutes passed where Eva dared not to move and the room came to a standstill once more. Wiping her hands against the sides of her dress, she took slow, deep breaths to try and calm her nerves that jangled with tension.

Having never chosen to become a mother, an inherent fear that she would grow to resent her child had plagued many a sleepless night back in the early days at 'Station 12'. These very same thoughts now came flooding back for the first time in several months, each one colliding with the next in one mass of anxiety. What if the baby reminded her of her time in captivity and this stopped them from forging a bond? What if she was a terrible mother and failed to cope with the pressure? What if she fell in love with the child, only for the government to take them away? What if the baby fell victim to the harsh realities of violence and disease that plagued their world?

Pushing the worries that caused a feeling of

sickness deep in her gut to the back of her mind, she refused to consider the reality that her child was due to be born any day now until it was absolutely unavoidable. She had always consoled herself by saying she could only ever cross that bridge when it came; only now this provided little in the way of comfort considering the bridge seemed to be within plain sight.

Needing to find a suitable distraction, she remembered requesting to accompany her father on today's hunt and hastily made for the door. Both her mother and father stood in the kitchen. The backpack slung over his shoulder, the spear in his hand and the look on his face as he glanced at her all told that he had no intention whatsoever of waiting for Eva to accompany him.

"Were you leaving?" she asked, already knowing the answer.

"Yeah. I have to get going if I want to get back before sundown."

"I'll just grab some breakfast then."

"What?"

"I'm coming with you remember."

"Eva…"

"You know, I can pick some berries on the way or something. Let's just go."

She knew what was coming but made for the door anyway, the need to clear her mind all too pressing.

"I think you should give it a miss today Eva." said Alexandra, zipping up her husband's backpack after placing a bottle of water inside.

"I'm fine. I want to go. Besides, I promised."

"I'll let you off the hook, Eva." her father continued with a smile, "You're hardly in the condition to be running around in the woods."

"But you agreed."

"You were tired and I was humouring you. I didn't think you would actually come."

"Well, I meant it so we'd better get going." Eva's hand was on the door handle now. Her heart grew heavier with every word of discouragement from her parents, causing the need to escape the house and her worries even more immediate.

"You can help me here instead." said Alexandra, hoping an alternative plan may be the solution.

"No thanks. Really, I want to go. I could use the fresh air." Her lungs felt tight as she spoke. She knew exactly what was happening but she still utterly refused to accept it.

"And what if you get tired? Or we come into trouble and need to run? How do plan on doing that?"

"I'll be fine. We better go if we want to get back before sundown." Eva stared straight ahead at the door as she spoke, too afraid to see the determination in her parent's eyes yet already knowing she was fighting a losing battle.

"You can't come Eva. I'm putting my foot down now." Alistair's tone had changed to one of definitive authority.

"Please." Eva pleaded now, desperate to escape the strange and unfamiliar kind of fear that was working its way through her entire body.

"Another time. Maybe once the baby is born." he replied.

With those words, the walls seemed to close in around her. Turning to face the room, it spiralled out of focus just as her bedroom had done earlier. Through the chaos before her eyes and the beating drum in her ears again, her mother's voice somehow found its way in.

"Eva, what's wrong?"

Her father's arm was around her shoulders now, guiding her towards the sofa. Her bare feet suddenly felt wet, though her vision was still too impaired to even consider seeing why.

"Oh my God." Her mother's voice appeared again.

With that single phrase Eva's brain threw itself into some sort of emergency mode, drawing the sickening spinning to a halt. She was sitting on the sofa, her mother crouching before her, one hand on each of her daughter's knees. Her father was running to their bedroom and soon returned with a clean towel in his hands.

"I'm not ready." Eva managed to say at last, her eyes fixed on her mother's face, drained of all its colour.

"It's happening Eva. The baby's coming."

Chapter Twenty-Five

Eva's head was resting against the back of the sofa, tiny beads of sweat trickling down her flushed cheeks. Her father was kneeling beside her, not daring to allow his face to show the pain caused by the vice-like grip of his daughter's hand on his. With her steady voice full of encouragement and gentle hands ready to welcome the infant into the world, it would have been quite believable that Alexandra had made her living as a midwife before The Breakdown; she was a picture of calm and tranquillity. In reality of course she had never delivered a child before and was just as terrified as her daughter; questions, doubts and words of fear swirling around her head at a million miles an hour. All she could do was remember as best she could her own experiences of being in labour and use that experience to help her daughter in whatever way she could.

The indignity of having her parents be the ones to see her in this condition and deliver her baby soon left Eva, for the pain now consuming her mind and body were unlike anything she had ever experienced before. By the time the first hour of labour had passed, the two people by her side could have been anyone; all she could possibly desire was for the agony to subside and the ordeal to be over. Doing her best to breathe when instructed to do so and push on command, she urged herself on with the continual thought that each and every contraction took her one step closer to the end of this suffering.

After hours that felt like days, her mother's voice brought the sweet sight of salvation.

"It's nearly over Eva. Just one last push. Give it everything you've got."

Hunching forward and gritting her teeth, Eva willingly obliged. With one last push and a muffled scream, a feeling of immediate relief washed over her like a bucket of ice-cold water being tipped on her from above. Slumping back on the sofa and gasping for air, every muscle in her body released their pent up tension at once, equally as exhausted from the experience as her mind was.

The delicate scream that pierced the air confirmed the arrival of the baby.

"He's beautiful." Alistair's voice crackled, the

feelings of pride clear to hear.

"He?" asked Eva, straining her neck forward to try and catch a glimpse of the sight she had waited nine long months in anticipation to behold, whether for better or worse.

"It's a boy." There in her mother's arms, wrapped neatly in a crisp, white towel, was a pale and fragile looking baby. Her son, with his big blue eyes and small button nose was placed in her arms and all at once the pain was forgotten; not just the pain of the delivery but every feeling of fear, anger and longing from the last nine months were shattered into a thousand tiny pieces as they faded into the depths of her mind.

The cries soon subsided, both pairs of blue eyes meeting for the first time. His face the epitome of innocence and complete obliviousness to the world he would be forced to survive in, a single memory reformed and charged its way back into focus; the one she had tried the hardest to forget for as long as her brain would allow. The moment was now bittersweet for Eva, for she finally held her son in her arms, both mother and child very much alive and well, though this served only to remind her of the one person that had made this moment possible.

"Do you have a name for this little guy?" asked Alistair.

"Matthew." said Eva. "I want to name him

Matthew."

Chapter Twenty-Six

Calm returned to the house once more, the new mother cradling her son and gazing at him through tear stained eyes. Though baby Matthew was wrapped tightly in a fresh towel that smelled of the open air, he managed to wriggle one hand free and reach up towards Eva. Holding out a finger for him, he gripped it, his mere touch enough to send shivers running down her spine and a smile across her face.

They were going to need as much cloth and material as they could get their hands on for use as nappies and blankets. Thankfully, Alexandra had had the foresight to keep back some meat from Alistair's last two hunts and had only the day before mixed up some herbal tea sachets. Giving the supplies to her husband in a burlap sack, she sent him into town to trade, urging him to keep the news of the new arrival to within their circle of most trusted friends. If local guards caught wind of the first baby born within the district for several years, news would spread like wildfire and Eva would find herself tarnished with a celebrity status she simply could not afford to maintain.

Alistair soon set off and Alexandra immediately sprang into action. Fetching a bucket of water from the trough and warming it over the stove, she set about helping to clean up both mother and child. Once the room had been cleansed of all sodden linen, Eva had washed and changed into a fresh, pale blue dress and Matthew was bathed and swaddled in the last remaining towel, she and Alexandra both breathed a sigh that registered their feelings of great accomplishment.

They sat side by side in comfortable silence for what could easily have been several hours, equally drained both physically and emotionally from the events of the day. Matthew drifted in and out of a restless sleep but remained largely quiet throughout until at last the crying started in full force.

"At least that means his lungs are healthy." Eva joked.

"I guess it's time to feed this little bundle." said Alexandra, her voice strained with exhaustion and croaky from such prolonged silence.

"I can't put it off a little longer then, no?" Eva asked with a wry smile.

With only a little trepidation from both parties, Matthew was soon feeding from the breast of his mother. The sensation of warmth coursing through Eva's entire body was both the strangest and single most wonderful feeling she had ever experienced. In those moments, true and uncompromising love was all that she knew.

Once adequately satisfied by his first meal, Matthew soon drifted back to sleep in his mother's arms. It was not much longer before Alistair returned looking just as worn out as his wife and daughter. Being careful not to wake the baby from his slumber, he emptied the contents of the sack onto the table. Gone were the makeshift teabags and cuts of fresh meat and in their place were a whole bundle of blankets in an assortment of colours and sizes.

"Well done." said Alexandra, reaching up to kiss him on the cheek. She immediately began assessing the quality of each blanket, a renewal of energy coursing through her. Those that were deemed useful were neatly folded and placed in a pile at the end of the table. Those of an insufficient standard to perform their function as blankets were soon cut up to be put to use as nappies for baby Matthew.

While Alexandra busied about her new task, Alistair removed his boots with a groan and took a place on the sofa beside Eva. Gently stroking Matthew's forehead, he leaned in for his first proper look at his grandson.

"He looks like Tristan, you know." Alistair's voice was as full of sorrow as it was happiness.

"I thought so too." said Alexandra, peering up from behind a tatty, brown blanket with a grin. "It's the button nose."

As soon as they said it, Eva could see it too and immediately wondered why it had taken her so long to notice how strikingly her new born son resembled her late brother. The poignant moment consumed the room for several minutes, though the realisation soon brought further release from previous fears that had lingered in the darkest depths of Eva's mind ever since her impregnation; the baby took after her family. No longer was there the risk that her son would grow up to be not only an emotional but physical reminder of how he was conceived. Many restless nights in 'Station 12' had been haunted with images of a child that bore no resemblance to the family; a black sheep for more reasons than one. At least now when she looked at her son, she would instead be filled with memories and a longing for her older brother whom she missed desperately; painful perhaps but far better than the alternative.

"He would have made a great uncle." It was Alistair who broke the silence. "After all, he was always pretty protective of you."

They all laughed warmly and at that very

moment, Eva swore to herself that she would never allow her son to suffer the same fate as her brother or the kindly young boy for whom he was named. The world had been robbed of enough good souls over the years and it was her duty to protect this one. From then on, she was prepared to do anything for the sake of her child; only now was she well and truly a mother.

The sun had long since retreated behind its mountainous blanket for the evening and everyone soon agreed to retire to bed and recuperate from the stresses of the day. Alexandra had already prepared what was once a hand-woven laundry basket for use as a crib by lining it with her carefully selected blankets.

Placing Matthew gently in his new bed, Eva picked up the basket and made for her bedroom but not before turning one last time for a look at her own mother and father.

"Thank you." The simple words said all that her heart needed to and with that she entered her room and pushed the door shut behind her. With the basket placed by the side of her bed, she gazed down at her son, barely awake and ignorant to the world around him. Skin as pale as snow; eyes as deep and blue as the ocean; he was a Cole alright. Reaching down, she kissed him on his little, button nose before picking up the photograph by her bedside and kissing it on the spot where her brother stood, his smile as warm as she had always remembered it to be. Putting it back in its place on the shelf, she climbed onto her bed, not bothering to undress or even to slip under the blanket. Instead, she gazed over the edge at her now sleeping baby boy, one hand dangling down to delicately bush against his. It was in this very position that she soon drifted off to sleep herself.

Chapter Twenty-Seven

Having already been woken periodically throughout the night by the sound of Matthew's cries, Eva decided to rise far earlier than usual. The sun had not yet fully risen to illuminate the world; its tip only visible enough beyond the mountain tops to tinge the landscape with a subtle orange glow.

Sitting on the edge of the bed, Eva looked down at Matthew who was also now fully awake but thankfully not crying. Her father would likely be intending to hunt later today in order to replace the food supplies they had given away in exchange for blankets and so he needed to rest while he had the chance.

Alone with her son properly for the first time, it was neither scary nor uncomfortable as Eva had previously anticipated. Instead, it felt easy and natural. Just as she readied herself to scoop him up in her arms, the familiar sound of a strained purr reached her ears. Sure enough, Snowy soon jumped in through the open window for one of his intermittent visits. Immediately upon spotting the basket and its contents, the purrs stopped.

Eva smiled as she lifted the makeshift crib onto the bed and coaxed Snowy into taking a closer look. Hesitant and untrustworthy by his very nature, it was several minutes before the nervous cat dared to poke his coal-black nose over the edge and peer inside. Eyes wide and nostrils flaring, he took in this unexpected and intriguing sight. A few harmless gargles and groans from Matthew and Snowy soon determined that the new addition was of no threat. The purring quickly resumed and he soon turned his attention to Eva instead, nuzzling against her hand, yearning for attention. Indulging him only for a moment, she ruffled his fur and tickled his stomach as he rolled around on his back, savouring every touch.

With a smile and a kiss on the head, Eva turned from Snowy and picked up Matthew. As she made for the door, Snowy leapt from the window and returned to the cover of the trees. Satisfied that Eva was still close by, their brief encounter was enough to reassure him and without any further attention from her, he deemed there to be no other reason to stay for now.

Entering the kitchen, Eva was surprised to see both of her parents already sitting at the table.

"What are you doing up so early?" she asked. "Matthew didn't wake you did he?"

"No, no. We were awake anyway." replied her father, dark circles under his eyes and mug of freshly brewed herbal tea in his hands.

"How did you sleep?" asked her mother.

"Not bad actually. I got more than I thought I would."

"And the little one?" she asked as she took him into her own arms for a hug.

"Pretty well."

"Did you feed him through the night?"

"Just once."

"He'll be hungry then. Get him fed and I'll fix you some breakfast."

Once both mother and child were full, he with his mother's milk and she with eggs collected from the hens in the yard, Alistair bid them all farewell and left for a day of hunting.

Eva and Alexandra filled their day by washing the now sorted blankets, ready for use and prepping the vegetable stew for the evening's supper. Eva tended to Matthew when need be; pinning the homemade nappies into place, comforting him when he cried and tucking him in for a nap whenever he seemed tired. Never in her life had she taken to something so quickly as she had motherhood and while she busied herself caring for her son, Alexandra scavenged several bunches of herbs from the edge of the woods and brewed batches of her teas to replace those they had used to trade.

Throughout the day, they laughed and smiled as they retold stories from the happier times in the past; of when Tristan got his first crush on a girl and how utterly infatuated he was; about how Eva had been so desperately attached to her teddy bear named Buttons and how Alistair used to take the whole family on camping trips in the woods that only he enjoyed but how the others had never had the heart to tell him otherwise.

No happy memory in this world was spared from being marred by a tinge of sadness however. Tristan was gone, his childhood crush more than likely also dead by now; Buttons had been left behind during their panicked attempt to flee the city at the outbreak of The Breakdown and family holidays were a thing of the past. With the arrival of baby Matthew however, this day became the first in a long time that they would be able to look back on in years to come and smile about, just as they did with these memories. This inner warmth allowed them for once to focus purely on the good times and not to be saddened by how unattainable the past now often seemed. Even if just for a few hours, they were finally able to forget just how much their lives had changed from then until now.

The return of Alistair brought the day abruptly back into the present and with it the stark reality of their current situation. One rabbit was all he had to show for his long day in the woods. Within a matter of minutes it was skinned, gutted, chopped and cooked through the stew. Though it provided a highly satisfying meal, it meant another day of trekking and searching through the undergrowth for Alistair, the thought of which soon coaxed him into bed to make sure he could recuperate beforehand.

The following day followed much the same routine as the previous one and once again Alistair returned in the evening with a poor bounty to show for his efforts, despite being gone for far longer than usual. Another rabbit and one small bird, the breed of which Eva was unfamiliar with, were all he had to offer when normally a hunt of that length would have amounted to at least double that level of bounty. The rabbit was prepared and boxed up for use the following day, while the bird was plucked, the cooked meat shredded and mixed through with a few carrots.

The third day Eva spent walking around the garden with Matthew in her arms, telling him all about the trees and the wondrous animals that lived in them. When her father emerged from them in the evening, they were grateful for the previous day's rabbit as his hunting sack was empty. In spite of an entirely unsuccessful hunt, he looked exhausted and Eva quickly became concerned.

Following their particularly lean meal that evening, Eva put Matthew down to sleep in his basket on the sofa and joined her mother and father at the table.

"Do you think the animals are dying out?" she asked, her question aimed at them both equally.

"What?" replied her father, his elbows propped on the table and head resting in his hands. The circles under his eyes had turned a deep shade of purple while the whites of his eyes themselves were so badly bloodshot, they appeared almost entirely red.

"Maybe they're migrating. I mean, animals adapt to their environment so maybe they've wizened on to the hunters around this area."

When her only response came in the form of a vacant expression on her father's face, she continued.

"Pickings have been pretty slim recently I mean." she said, as though to clarify exactly the reasoning behind her original question.

"Yeah. Maybe." he replied.

"I think you should get some sleep Alistair." said Alexandra in a warm and caring tone.

"Yeah, I'm just tired. I'll get some sleep and… tomorrow. I'll catch more tomorrow."

Without any further conversation, Alistair bid them goodnight with a simple nod and left for bed. When Eva's eyes met her mother's for a brief moment, Alexandra quickly looked away, rising from her seat and busying herself with the dishes that were steeping in a bucket of warm water on the counter.

From then, Eva knew for sure; they were hiding something from her. It was not the fact that something was wrong that scared her most but the thought that whatever it was her own parents deemed it so bad they were keeping it from her. Was her father ill? Was he even spending his days in the woods?

With too many thoughts and questions to process all at once, Eva decided not to press her mother on the matter for now. Doing her very best not to let her concern show on her face, she chatted as normal for an hour or so before Alexandra also bid her goodnight and left the room.

Once alone, the questions crept their way back in. Just what were they hiding from her and for how long did they intend to keep her in the dark? Should she ask them directly about what was going on or was she better off trusting their judgement and leaving well alone?

Having spent the last nine months embroiled in secrets and lies, she soon came to the conclusion that no matter the issue at hand, she would rather know and be able to face it head on. Just as she resolved to find out the truth the following morning, the faded sound of an engine appeared. A moment later, a bright light shone in through the kitchen window and the sound of the engine came to an abrupt halt. Visitors were not common these days, particularly not at this hour.

With a glance at a soundly sleeping Matthew, Eva crossed the room, crouching so as not to be seen through the window. She peered over the frame just as Snowy had done the basket and just like he before her, she soon relaxed.

At the end of the yard, Declan was climbing out of his truck. Hoping not to awaken her father, who evidently for whatever reason was gravely in need of a good night's sleep, Eva opened the door and began to cross the garden to meet him, the cold grass brushing against her bare feet as she walked.

"Sorry to just turn up like this." Declan whispered as he spoke, obviously aware of the inappropriateness of the time at which he had chosen to call.

"That's okay." Eva answered in an equally hushed tone. "Do you need something?"

"No, I just came to drop this off. It's the stuff

your father asked for. He said he wanted it right away." he said, holding out a package wrapped in brown paper and secured with string.

"Right. Yeah, I'll pass it on to him." she answered, taking the package and hoping not to look as though she had no idea what he was talking about, in spite of the fact that this was very much the case.

"Congratulations on the baby." said Declan, adorned with that same warm smile as the day he had driven her home.

Though for a brief moment she panicked that news had already spread around town, she soon realised that her significantly slimmer frame was more than a giveaway that she had by now given birth. Besides, if her father had called him in for a favour, that means he can be trusted and no one can smile so sincerely and not mean it.

"Thanks and thank you for this, I'll be sure and give it to him."

"No problem."

"I'd invite you in but…"

"Oh, that's okay. It's late."

"Yeah. Maybe another time."

"Sure. Yeah. Well, goodnight."

"Night."

With another smile, Declan turned and quickly climbed back into his truck. By the time Eva had returned to the house, he had gone; the headlights faded into the darkness; the sound of the engine swallowed by the night.

After another quick look at Matthew, still fast asleep, she placed the package on the table. Though every fibre of her body told her not to, she could not resist opening it. Taking care not to tear the paper, she delicately untangled the string holding it in place and unfolded the packaging. Uncovering a tatty, cardboard box, she lifted its lid and exposed the contents.

The small sachet of painkillers, box of matches and bandages would not have seemed so alarming if by their side were not the handgun and red box full of bullets. Suddenly the secret her parents were keeping from her seemed a lot more frightening.

Chapter Twenty-Eight

Eva quickly re-wrapped the package and tied the string in place once more; being sure to leave no evidence that it had ever been opened. Leaving it on the table, she picked up the basket, which still contained an oblivious Matthew and hurried to her bedroom. Her heart was pounding against her ribcage now, each breath shorter and faster than the last.

Laying the basket on her bed, Matthew awoke with a jolt, his eyes swivelling frantically to try and take in his surroundings. Within seconds, he was screeching, the noise battering Eva's eardrums. Had it not been so late at night and her nerves not been so shaken, the screams would not have perturbed her but she hastily scooped him into her arms and cradled him, gently hushing and swaying to and fro to try and resettle him before her parents came to investigate or offer assistance. Having just discovered what she had, she knew she would be entirely incapable of hiding the multitude of questions and worries from boldly displaying themselves across her face. She needed time to think; to allow this latest revelation to sink in.

What were they planning? Why would they need a gun? How had her father possibly afforded one? How did Declan manage to find it?

Guns were not common these days; not among civilians anyway. The government's guards were often armed with rifles and handguns but all others had been recalled when the riots broke out. Though at first many refused to hand them in, people become more and more obedient as the already sparse population continued to plummet towards extinction. Before long, only a few rogue weapons remained in circulation; incredibly valuable on the black market, hugely helpful for unskilled hunters yet incredibly dangerous if you were ever caught withholding one. By now, possession of a firearm would almost certainly entail death. What was so important that her father would be willing to risk his life for?

Eva looked down at the scar on her leg and ran her fingers across the patch of hard, tapered skin. The sound of the gunshot that could so easily have ended her life replayed in her mind. The image of Thomas Cain's cold, hard stare as his hand griped his rifle soon followed.

Holding out Matthew and looking into his eyes, the moment of his namesake's death also began to repeat itself again and again, the sound of the final bullet leaving the gun louder every time. It was the first time she had allowed herself to relive the memory in full since she had departed from his impromptu burial ground. Allowing the overwhelming feelings of guilt and regret to consume her only for a few fleeting seconds, she locked them away in the back of her mind once more; relying once again on this now invaluable skill.

Holding back the tears, she held Matthew close and began to rock him from side to side. Her mind was made up. She hated guns. She utterly reviled them and everything they represented. Tomorrow, she would get the truth out of her parents once and for all.

Baby soothed; his tears wiped away by his mother's bare hands, a feeling of calm and clarity seeped its way back into the room. Figuring it best to question her father alone, Eva resolved to accompany him on the following day's hunting trip whether he wanted her to or not. Not only would she see how he had really been spending his time away from home over the past few days but they could talk for hours just as they had done when Eva had been a young child. Hoping that sooner or later he was bound to let his guard down and the truth to slip out, she wanted to give him one last chance to be honest with her. If not, she would be forced to drag it out of him herself by whatever means necessary but one thing was for sure; Eva's life had been dictated and influenced more than enough by secrets in the past and she was no longer prepared to let others control her fate; however good intentioned their actions were. Tomorrow, she would learn the truth.

Chapter Twenty-Nine

Eva was the first one to wake the following morning. In fact, she had barely slept at all. She had woken sporadically at almost every hour; drifting in and out of dreams that were a mixture of fantasy and memory; all of which involved guns, violence and suffering. Grateful for the distraction of having to feed Matthew on two occasions, she eventually found herself unable and unwilling to drift off anymore. Wanting to be certain she would not miss her father before he departed, she decided it best to save herself the risk of any further nightmares by readying herself for the no doubt long day ahead.

She dressed in a simple, plain white dress with embroidered detailing around the neckline that came to rest at her knees. Well aware that a dress was far from ideal hunting gear, she chose it regardless, not wishing to contend with the discomfort of squeezing into her old jeans that would inevitably still be ill fitting following her pregnancy. At least this way, the white of the garment would match the blossom now flourishing upon the tips of the trees, allowing her to blend in somewhat with the environment if her father was closing in on any potential prey. Somehow, she doubted they would be hunting at all; not if Alistair decided to divulge whatever secrets he had been keeping.

She pulled on her old, brown leather brogues; the sturdiest footwear she owned and her trusted hunting shoes. She had been wearing them the day they stumbled upon Snowy and had considered them a good luck charm ever since. Though they had since become at least a size too small, they remained the best shoes she had. She made sure to pull the laces tight and secure them neatly in place, not wanting the shoes to rub against the heels of her feet as she walked; blisters were a hunter's worst enemy and her previous ones from her escape through the forest had only just healed.

While she dressed, Matthew whimpered and grew increasingly agitated, wriggling until his arms were free from his blanket and grasping at the air around him. Lifting him out of his crib and whispering softly in his ear, his irritation was quelled before it escalated into screams and tears, something for which Eva was very grateful. Though she knew today was the day she would confront her father and uncover his secrets, she hoped for a little while longer to settle the butterflies that fluttered violently around her stomach.

Entering the kitchen, her eyes were immediately drawn to the brown package that still sat where she had left it the previous evening. She could hear her heart beating in her ears again. The mere presence of the gun was enough to make her feel uneasy. Her father had never used one even for hunting purposes, why now would he ask for one to be delivered in secret?

Shaking herself free from the growing tension that snaked its way through her muscles, she took a seat on the sofa, feeding Matthew before laying him down and smiling at him as she shook the homemade rattle her mother had made. Fashioned from an old tin filled with dried grains with an old piece of cloth stitched around it, it was the nearest thing to a toy they had been able to offer him.

Once Matthew grew disinterested in the game, Eva stood and walked to the counter by the window, taking a handful of fresh berries that sat in a bowl and slipping each one into her mouth one by one. As her teeth pierced the skin, sweet purple juices burst free and overwhelmed her taste buds with more flavour than they had experienced for weeks. Her mother must have gathered them, as though her father could usually be relied upon to source meat, it was Alexandra who knew which herbs, fruits and other natural produce could be trusted for consumption. Following the various diseases that had spread during The Breakdown, several normally reliable crops had become lethal for humans, with people having to adapt quickly to their ever dwindling food supply. Having been handpicked and washed, ready for eating by her mother, Eva had no hesitation in sampling these particular berries however.

She gazed out of the window as she ate, the sun only just beginning to emit its familiar glow and bring the world back to life.

"I must have gotten up earlier than I thought." she said to herself in a whisper.

Butterflies largely subdued in thanks to a full belly, Eva began to pace the room, occasionally glancing down at Matthew and pulling a strange face to try and keep him entertained. Eventually, a door opened and Alistair and Alexandra entered the room.

"Morning." said Eva without a smile.

"Morning." replied her mother, "You're up awfully early, aren't you?"

"I couldn't really sleep. Besides, Matthew was awake so I figured I'd just get up."

"And how is the little man?" asked Alistair. Evidently feeling better after a solid sleep, the circles under his eyes were now a lighter shade of lilac as opposed to the deep purple of the day before.

"He's good. Really good actually. He's barely cried at all."

"You got lucky with this one, that's for sure." said Alexandra, leaning down to kiss Matthew's forehead.

"I was thinking I would come out hunting with you today, Dad?" The question escaped her lips before she had time to consider otherwise, sounding more forward than she had hoped it would.

"What?" Alistair replied.

"I'm not sure that's a good idea Eva. You should still be taking it easy and Matthew's not exactly able to go trekking through the woods with you, is he?" Alexandra spoke before Eva had time to reply.

"I could do with getting out the house for a bit. I thought maybe you could watch Matthew for me. Come on, for old times' sake." she said, managing to force a smile and sound genuinely excited as she spoke.

Alistair and Alexandra exchanged a fleeting glance and opting to act before they had time to resist her request any further, Eva sprang into action.

"That's settled then. I've already eaten so you get some breakfast and I'll gather some water and meet you out front. Thanks Mum."

Leaning forward, she kissed Matthew on the

nose.

"Be good for Grandma."

She scooped up her father's hunting bag, which sat by the side of the sofa and headed for the front door. Perhaps in shock at how quickly the situation had changed, or frozen with fear that their secret was about to be exposed, neither Alistair nor Alexandra moved from where they stood or uttered a single word.

Just before pulling the door closed behind her, Eva turned and pointed towards the table.

"Oh and Dad, I meant to say, Declan dropped that parcel off for you last night. See you in a minute."

Once the door was shut, she breathed a sigh of relief at how smoothly the operation had gone. The cool morning breeze was a welcome reprieve from the simmering heat that had flushed her cheeks. She quickly made her way to the back of the house and opened the front pocket of her father's bag, removing the plastic bottle he always kept inside so she could replenish its depleted water supply from the trough.

Once the bottle was full, sealed and tucked away in its usual compartment once more, she pulled the straps of the bag around her shoulders and onto her back then returned to the front of the house. Her father was already waiting. Eva wondered if perhaps his own nerves at being exposed had kept him from eating breakfast. Either way, she was now eager to head off.

"Shall we get going then?" she asked.

"Sure. Let's go."

The sun was now high in the sky, bright enough to weave its way through the trees and illuminate their path but still early enough in the day to uncover some unsuspecting animals. After a twenty minute walk with nothing more than general small talk, both Alistair and Eva fell into silence. Though this was normal during a hunt so as not to scare away any nearby animals concealed in the undergrowth, it felt unusually uncomfortable on this particular morning. By now, they were deep in the forest that surrounded their remote home with Eva finding it strangely pleasant to be surrounded by trees once again; the chirp of birds and scurrying of mice now welcomingly familiar.

By the time the first hour had passed, the bag on Eva's back contained two rabbits, a small bird with brown plumage and a squirrel. The thought of dead animals being so close to her body made her skin prickle with discomfort. Eva had never been much of a hunter herself; more a companion to keep her father company during the long days in the woods. Her father had attempted to teach her how to throw knives several years ago and though her aim and technique quickly improved, once the time came to make the transition from hitting trees as target practice to actually killing animals, she quickly lost interest in the activity. In fact, in all the years she had been accompanying her father during his hunts, not once had she ever made a kill by her own hands and even to this day, she felt a pang of sadness with each lifeless body she scooped up and placed into the bag, being sure to whisper a brief apology to the animal as she did so.

Mid-afternoon soon descended and the two came to rest on a fallen tree. Eva was reluctant at first, the sight threatening to release some memories she simply could not afford to relive right now but she quickly swallowed back her hesitation and took a seat beside her father.

"It's been a pretty successful hunt today." said Eva, handing her father the bottle of water.

"Yeah, it's been good."

"Why do you think it's been so quiet the last few days?"

"I don't know." he said, taking hurried sips between each exchange.

"There must be a reason. Seems a little odd we've managed to get so much today when you've struggled all week."

"Maybe you're my lucky charm." He smiled as he spoke but didn't turn to look at her.

"What was in the package?" she asked; her desire for answers becoming too powerful to resist any longer.

"Just some medical supplies. I figured we should stock up, just to be on the safe side now that little Matthew is here."

"Nothing else?" she asked, offering up his final chance to come clean.

"No. That's all."

Eva felt her heart sink with his words. Of all the people left in the world and after everything they had been forced to overcome as a family, she never thought her own parents would shut her out this much.

"Why are you lying to me?" she asked.

"What?"

"You're lying. I know you are." Her voice grew louder with each word as anger coursed its way through her veins.

"I'm not. What is…"

"The gun? When were you going to tell me about that?"

"You opened it?"

"You've been acting strange for days, both of you: Dodging questions; telling lies and disappearing all day with barely a catch to show for it. How do you think it feels being kept in the dark by my own family? After everything that's happened. After everything I've been through to get home."

By now Eva was on her feet. Her face a deep shade of red; hands clenched into fists; her nails slowly cutting into her palms. Alistair lifted his head and looked his daughter in the eyes for the first time all day; his own covered in a veil of tears.

"I'm sorry." he said, "You're right. It's time I showed you what's really going on."

Chapter Thirty

In silence, Eva followed her father through the woodland, her heart beating faster and louder with every step. The density of the trees soon began to recede and the noise of running water reached Eva's ears.

"The ocean?" she asked.

"Yeah. It's not far now."

Alistair progressed with certainty, showing not a single sign of hesitation whatsoever. Wherever he was leading her, clearly this was a place he had visited several times before. Exiting the cover of the forest at last, the lush greens were replaced by the pale greys and pastel blues of the rocks that mingled with the golden sands. The entire landscape before them was surrounded by towering cliffs with dangerously pointed edges. Birds dove from the peaks and plunged into the icy cold waters in the hunt for what little fish still inhabited the depleted waters.

Straining her eyes to follow the naturally formed pathway into the valley below, Eva saw two things that instilled equal levels of fear; a man and a boat.

"I'm sorry we didn't tell you. We just didn't want to worry you." said Alistair, his voice not powerful enough to draw his daughter's focus away from this latest disclosure.

"Tell me what?" she asked, her voice broken by doubt and her eyes still very much fixed on the man hunched over the evidently handmade, wooden structure by the shoreline.

"They're coming for you Eva. For all of us."

This time she managed to pull her gaze from where it had been so transfixed and look into the worried face of her father; eyes wide, brow furrowed, lips pursed.

"What do you mean?" she asked.

"Government presence has been growing in town and rumours have spread fast. We have to leave this place."

"But… I thought you said they wouldn't come after me anymore? That we were safe here?"

"Your mother and I, we didn't want to scare you. You've been through so much already that we thought you deserved at least a few days of happiness; a chance to feel safe and free."

"But I'm not."

"No. Not yet anyway."

"So who is…?" her eyes returned to the man by the edge of the water, still unaware of their presence.

"Declan. He's been helping me prepare. In exchange I said he could come with us."

"Come with us? Come with us where?" Eva's voice was growing louder as fear coursed through her system once more.

"As far from here as we can. We need to expose this government for what they truly are once and for all."

"And so your solution is to sail away, off into the sunset to live happily ever after?" Anger too was pushing its way to the forefront, as Eva's cheeks flushed red.

"We can work our way along the shoreline until we get to a nearby stretch of land that looks safe. Then we can resupply and form a plan from there. But if we have to keep sailing, then yes, that's exactly what we'll do." Alistair's voice remained calm with every word; his plan having clearly been meticulously formed in his mind for days.

"So this is why you've been coming home practically empty handed all week? You've been building this boat?"

"Yes."

"And why you and mum have been so on edge

with me?"

"Yes."

Eva had to admire his eventual, blunt honesty. Though she remained frustrated at having been kept in the dark from the plan that revolved around her own safety, the enormity of the situation began to dilute any blame almost at once.

"Can I see it?"

"Sure."

Eva moved to take a step towards the shore when her father's arm blocked her way.

"Hold on." he said. Lifting his fingers to his mouth, he whistled two, slow tones followed by one much shorter and higher in register. He repeated this phrase and as he did so, Declan stood up straight, turned in the direction of the noise and performed the same brief tune in return.

"Just our little way of letting each other know we're here and the coast is clear. We don't want those security guards following us down here." Alistair explained the strange ritual before gesturing for Eva to continue her way down the path. The wind howled off the water as waves crashed against the rocks.

Declan soon spotted the duo and began to walk towards them, that now familiar smile spread across his face again.

"Good to see you Eva. I figured you'd be here

sooner or later." he said.

"Can't say I was expecting it so much myself." she replied in jest to her father. Her temples were pounding against her skull and her mouth was bone dry from the headache that had gripped hold of her like a vice.

"The boat's almost ready." said Alistair, "We just need to finish the sail but that shouldn't take long. Declan's already prepared the wood, so all we need is another sheet or a blanket to reinforce it. We should be ready to leave tomorrow."

"Tomorrow?" repeated Eva, "This is all happening so fast. I… What about Matthew?"

"I know you're scared Eva but we can do this." He put his hands on his daughter's shoulders as he spoke and leaned in close, both fixing their eyes on those of the other. "Once we're out of here, we can let the world know what's really going on behind closed doors in this God forsaken country. You'll finally be free of them."

"But I…"

"You can stop other women going through what you have. You can stop other children from being born into a life on the run."

His final words struck Eva's heart like a drum. Her vision blurring from tears, her gaze remained on her father's face. Never had she seem him more determined or more certain of anything in her whole life.

"Okay." she said, "Let's do it. Let's get out of here."

"Okay." said Alistair, managing a fleeting smile through his obvious tension.

"But I want to leave as soon as possible. I can't stay here another night knowing we're in danger."

Alistair stood up straight and looked over at Declan, who had been standing uncomfortably idle during their exchange.

"Can we be ready to leave by tonight?" he asked.

"Sure." said Declan, "The boat itself is ready. All we need is a sheet for the sail."

"Then it's settled. We leave tonight. You get everything sorted here and we'll go back and get Alexandra and Matthew. We'll see if we can find a sheet and meet you back here in a couple of hours."

Eva felt a surge of adrenaline coursing through her body as her father was speaking. Just minutes ago, she had been entirely unaware of his grand plan; now, she would be leaving her home behind within a couple of hours and never looking back.

"I'm on it." said Declan, "Be careful though. The market was crawling with security this morning; even more than yesterday."

As though an invisible timer had been set off, Alistair grabbed hold of Eva's arm and began to run back up the rocky pathway. Already struggling for air by the time they reached the treeline, they plunged themselves back into the clutches of Mother Nature.

A mere few metres into the depths of the forest and Alistair came to an immediate halt causing Eva to collide into his back. Both were breathing heavily and soon it became all too clear that something was wrong. No birds chirped; no leaves rustled; the sound of their aching lungs was all that was to be heard. Eva quickly recalled her first encounter with the men from 'Station 12' following her escape all those weeks ago. Alistair turned to face Eva, his hand taking hold of hers.

"Dad?"

Before he could answer, a shot rang out, louder than any that had been haunting her dreams for the past months. A spray of red assaulted Eva's white dress as Alistair fell to the ground. Still gripping onto his daughter's hand, she fell with him, landing on her knees by his side. A gaping wound tore through his stomach. Time seemed to slow to a standstill as the world around them disappeared. Alistair's hand lost its grip on Eva's and her horrified gaze met his just long enough for her to see the light leave her father's eyes.

Chapter Thirty-One

Numbed to everything, Eva ran. Branches scraped at her skin as she fled the scene. Shards of bark flew past her face, blown from their trees by menacing bullets. She tried desperately to clear her mind of the fog that had descended upon it so as to allow her to remember the way which she and her father had come.

Stumbling upon the fallen tree at which they had rested not an hour ago, she knew at least she was heading in the right direction. Muffled shouts could be heard from behind, blocked in part by the tribal like pounding of her heart in her chest. She did not dare to look back.

Weaving in and out of the trees like a doe fleeing a hunter, being no longer with child meant that she was lighter on her feet than she had been during previous chases and she soon put distance between herself and her pursuers. With the beautifully innocent face of her son breaking its way through the mist, she had all the motivation she needed to press on in spite of the pain that shot through her legs. She had to reach her house before the soldiers did. The possibility that they had already arrived there was one she simply did not allow herself to consider.

Animals fled the scene in a panic as she tore her way through the forest. After twenty minutes with no falter in the speed at which she ran, Eva broke through the treeline that surrounded her home. Slamming against the door, she threw it open to find the kitchen empty of life.

"Mum!" she remained in the open doorway as she called, her chest heaving with exhaustion; lungs desperate for oxygen.

A moment later, Alexandra appeared at the door to her bedroom.

"Eva? What's wrong? Where's your father?"

"We have to go now. Where's Matthew?"

"I put him down for a nap in your room. Eva, what's going on?" the panic on her mother's face was clear to see.

Eva ran into her bedroom. On the bed, Matthew slept in the basket that had served as his crib for the past week. Scooping him up into her arms, blanket and all, as gently as her adrenaline fuelled body would allow, she granted herself only a moment's pause to glance one last time at the picture that sat upon the shelf by her bed: Young, happy and free; her now depleted family before The Breakdown; before this nightmare ever started.

Alexandra followed her daughter into the room, eyes now wild with fear.

"Eva, will you tell me what is going on? Where is your father?"

"He's dead." said Eva, her voice void of emotion and brain still numbed to the reality of the words she spoke.

Alexandra fell back and gripped the doorframe to stop from falling. Her jaw hung open and her eyelids fluttered.

"Wh… How?"

"They're here. The men from 'Station 12'. They've come for us."

Alexandra did not alter her position.

"Mum, we don't have time. We have to get to the boat."

"The boat?" asked Alexandra, her hands still clasped around the doorframe for support.

"Dad told me everything. Mum, we have to go now."

A single tear made its way down Alexandra's left cheek. With a nod, she steadied herself and turned back towards the kitchen. Eva followed, eyes fixed straight ahead the whole time, afraid of what may happen if she allowed herself the time to say farewell to the place she had called home for so many years; the place she had so desperately longed to return to during her months in captivity; the place she must now leave behind forever.

There was no time to hunt for a makeshift sail; the boat would simply have to do without and though the thought of the gun that sat in the box upon the table made a brief appearance in her mind, Eva refused to equip herself with even the mere possibility of resorting to the same measures as her pursuers.

By the time they had reached the treeline once more, both had broken into a gentle run. Matthew was jostled awake and began to whimper but Eva soothed him with kisses and words of comfort as they pressed on.

Without time to explain that they must take a detour so as to avoid the oncoming security personnel, Eva simply led her mother in a loop around the way in which she had come just moments earlier, her natural instinct and familiarity with navigating the forests of the earth guiding her on her way as they both forced their exhausted bodies through the thick undergrowth, calling on every ounce of fight they had left to give. Without time for any form of discussion or debate, Eva's only goal was to reach the boat and flee their hunters, seeing out her father's plan. Before long, they had reached the edge of the trees that looked out on to the coastline; the towering cliffs all around. Knowing there was no time for an emotional farewell, it pained Eva not to tell her mother that her father's body was laid just metres away behind the surrounding shrubbery but it was a decision she deemed utterly necessary if they hoped to escape while fear and adrenaline still fuelled their actions.

Gesturing for her mother to stop, Eva peered out of the trees and her heart immediately sank. Men, dressed in black with guns in hand waited along the path to where Alistair and Declan's boat was. Then it struck her. Declan had waited on the beach and had been preparing the boat for departure. Straining back she did her best to mimic the three toned whistle her father had done on her first visit here what now felt like days ago. After a brief pause and a confused glance from her mother, the sound returned to them; Declan was still alive and was waiting for them on the beach, the sound of the gunshot that killed her father providing the warning he needed to conceal himself and evade capture.

A confusing mixture of relief and panic washed over Eva. She and her mother were not alone in their efforts but how could they possibly slip by the soldiers? Even if they managed, what use was escape if their pursuers knew exactly where they were headed and could merely continue to follow them? Just as questions began to overwhelm her mind once again, a single voice cleared all else from consideration. It was her father's, and it repeated one of the last and most important things he had ever said to her.

"You can stop other children from being born into a life on the run."

A life on the run; this was what faced Eva and Matthew for as long as they lived. However long they continued to flee, the men from 'Station 12' would merely pursue them. They would not rest until the escapees were dead and the truth about what happened in the dark cells of 'Station 12' had died with them.

Gripped by a sudden sense of calm and clarity, Eva looked into her mother's eyes. Without exchanging a single word, they both understood exactly what was about to happen. Breaking away from her mother's desperate and pleading stare before she could attempt to change her mind, she looked down at her son and did all she could to hold back her tears as she kissed him on the forehead.

"I love you." she whispered.

Minutes later, Eva ran from the cover of the trees to the immediate sound of panic from the surrounding soldiers.

"There she is!" a voice cried out.

Eva did not run for the beach but instead headed up the steep slope to the right of the path that led to the top of the nearest cliff. She gripped the delicate bundle in her arms tighter than ever, the end of the blanket flowing in the wind behind as she ran. The air soon became stifling as the icy breeze threatened to topple her. Sharp, protruding rocks made the journey difficult as she jumped, stumbled and ran as fast as her greatly depleted body could manage. The sound of thundering footsteps growing ever louder was all that pushed her onwards, the soldiers very much in pursuit.

Reaching the cliff edge and sliding to a halt, Eva's heart ached with the enormity of what she now knew she must do. Turning to face her adversaries, of which there were at least a dozen, she found they had already formed a semi-circular barrier around her, leaving no option to turn back now. Their eyes red with rage, murder was all that was on their minds as they lifted their weapons and took aim. The men of 'Station 12' had unwittingly created a vessel for the truth and now they must see out its elimination. Eva's white dress, still splattered red with her own father's blood, fluttered around her trembling knees. Shutting her eyes tightly, the tears were stopped. Her skin prickled, blood rushing through her veins at a rate like never before. Birds called in distress from beyond the treeline and soon circled overhead.

Without time to picture the faces of those lost along the way or those she must now leave behind, Eva leaned back over the edge of the cliff. Gone from the sights and the clutches of the armed soldiers, she was hurtling silently towards her end. The power of the air that swirled around her body forced her arms to open and from the blanket tumbled a handful of twigs and branches. In that final moment, eyes reopening to face the sky above, a smile spread across her face. For the first and last time in years, Eva was truly free. More importantly, she had saved her son from the grasp of his would be killers, winning him the right to live his life. Crashing into the lapping waves below, everything went dark and at once it was over; Nature reclaimed the body of its own vessel.

Beneath the cliffs, a lone boat sailed out towards the looming sunset: Declan at the helm, a makeshift oar gripped tightly in his hands; Alexandra at the back, cradling her crying grandson, his big blue eyes wide to the world as tears streamed silently down her face. With all that remained of her family now held in her arms, her heart was plagued with a sorrow she knew would never leave but her spirit was equally roused by a determination to raise Matthew in the memory of his mother. It was this unlikely trio that were now tasked with exposing their twisted government's actions to the world and ensuring that neither Eva Cole's name nor her sacrifice would ever be forgotten.

Printed in Great Britain
by Amazon.co.uk, Ltd.,
Marston Gate.